Anonymous

Hamilton

The Birmingham of Canada

Anonymous

Hamilton
The Birmingham of Canada

ISBN/EAN: 9783337186494

Printed in Europe, USA, Canada, Australia, Japan

Cover: Foto ©Andreas Hilbeck / pixelio.de

More available books at **www.hansebooks.com**

The City Hall.

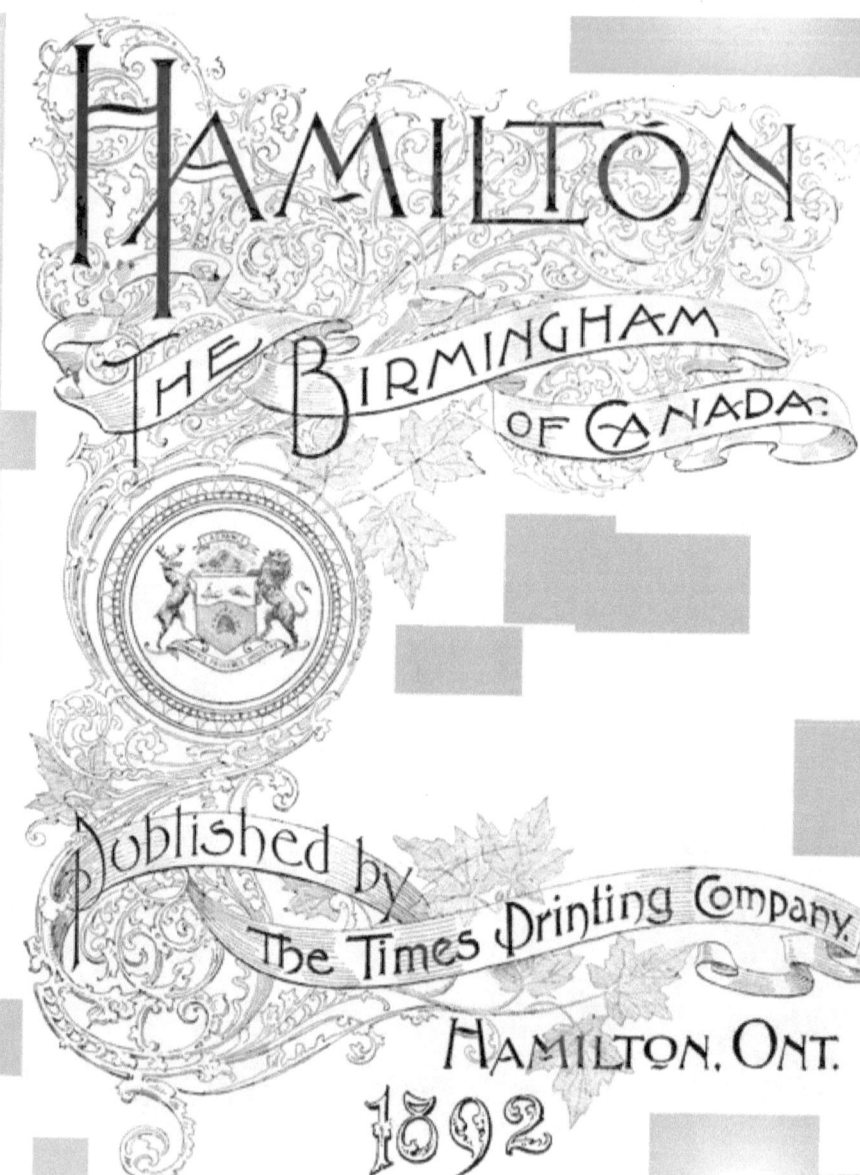

HAMILTON

The Birmingham of Canada

Published by The Times Printing Company.

HAMILTON, ONT.

1892

HAMILTON
THE BIRMINGHAM OF CANADA

IN the month of August, 1889, the City of Hamilton devoted a week to holding a Grand Carnival.

By an accidental missing of a train at Niagara Falls for New York, a party of English gentlemen, who had been on a tour through Canada and the United States, were induced to take the run of forty miles from Niagara to Hamilton, to kill the time while awaiting the departure of the next train going East. So much struck were they with the city, its position, its beauty and resources, that what was intended to be a visit of a few hours became several weeks, and, on their arrival back in England, they wrote to the Secretary of the Hamilton Board of Trade, informing him of the circumstances above recorded, and added: "Of all the places we had visited during our trip on the American Continent, the prettiest, cleanest, healthiest, and best conducted was the City of Hamilton, Canada; and from our inspection of the vast and varied manufacturing industries, its one hundred and seventy factories, with its 14,000 artisans, the large capital invested, and the immense output annually, we concluded it was well named the Birmingham of Canada, and has undoubtedly a great and glorious future before it." The letter finished with the query? "If we saw it by the accidental missing of a train, why not do something to call the attention of the outside world, so that people can go to your City and see for themselves its advantages?"

That letter has had much to do with the publishing of this Souvenir. The year 1893 will be a memorable one on this side of the Atlantic, the World's Fair at Chicago will attract tens of thousands of Europeans; and, perhaps, it would be safe to say that nine-tenths of the travel will be via Niagara Falls, and through Canada, either in going to or coming from Chicago, and very many from Great Britain, France and Germany, will want to do more than merely pass through this fair Province of Ontario, they will want to see some of our progressive cities, our magnificent scenery, our great lakes and waterways; and no place would combine the whole and give to the visitor more pleasure and enjoyment than a lay-off on their journey at the beautiful City of Hamilton, the third largest city in the Dominion, the second largest in the Province, and the prettiest and healthiest in America. With that end in view every effort has been put forth to give to the traveler an attractive Souvenir, with a brief review of the products and resources of Canada in general, and of this city in particular, so that capital and labor in the outside world may be able to judge and profit by information imparted by a recital of facts.

It has been the aim of the writer to give faithfully an outline of Hamilton as it is to-day, and avoid the customary review of what it was so many years ago.

In nearly every new town or city in the West, especially in the United States, very rapid strides have been made in a few years, and to boom the town has become a perfect science in the hands of skilful land agents—all good in its way—and generally starting out with "This City eight or ten years ago was a complete wilderness, etc. etc., and now it has a population of, etc., etc., and is, etc., etc., and must become the, etc., etc., etc.

We rather take the ground that Hamilton, has for many years been of steady growth, with no over-speculation, less failures, and less depreciation than any city in America: and its affairs to-day are on the most solid basis, with the most complete water works and sewer systems, both gas and electric lighting and an excellent electric railway to all parts of this town: and by both rail and water has direct communication and traffic with all parts of the world.

Manufacturing almost every article required for use in the Dominion, Hamilton is the great centre for skilled labor, and for public and high school education ranks first in Canada.

Hamilton—Western View from Mountain.

Hamilton—Central View from Mountain.

View on the Bay Front

HAMILTON, the second city in the Province of Ontario, is situated on the south shore of Hamilton (formerly Burlington) Bay, the western extremity of Lake Ontario. It lies just east of the 80th degree of longitude, and just north of the 43d parallel of latitude.

Hamilton occupies an alluvial plain lying between the bay and the escarpment which forms the outer rim of the lake basin. This escarpment—locally known as "the mountain"—is the height over which the Niagara plunges at the Falls. From its summit a magnificent view may be had. The city lies immediately below, the squares in the centre as distinct as those of a chess board, while in other parts the luxuriant maples with which the streets are lined, almost hide the dwellings from sight. The broad blue waters of Lake Ontario stretch away to the eastern horizon. To the northward the view is closed in by a continuation of the height on which the observer stands. The plain is covered in all directions with fruitful farms and dotted with thriving villages. The spires of Toronto may be dimly discerned on the north side of the lake, forty miles away; and on a clear day the smoke of Niagara, at about the same distance, may sometimes be seen.

Hamilton has a population of over 50,000 and is in direct railway communication with all parts of the Province, while she has by the great lakes and river water communication from Chicago, Duluth and Sault St. Marie at the west to the Atlantic seaboard.

The area of the city is 3,696 acres. There are ninety and a quarter miles of streets, forty miles of sewers, ninety and three-tenths miles of water mains, and thirty-five and a half acres of public parks.

The city is represented by two members in the Dominion Parliament and by one in the Ontario Legislature. It has three daily newspapers. Its local affairs are managed by a city council composed of a Mayor and twenty-one Aldermen. It is amply supplied with excellent water from Lake Ontario.

A police force of fifty men is found ample to preserve the peace, and a highly efficient fire department has been able to save the city from serious loss of fire. The streets are lighted by electric lamps.

No other Canadian city has won for itself the industrial celebrity that Hamilton has attained. The city is often called the Birmingham of Canada, and though comparison with the world's great work-shop in the English midlands is presumptuous, it is not altogether unwarranted. A place, within the memory of living men transformed from the wilds of a forest, can necessarily in but few things be compared with Birmingham. In one point, however, such a comparison may not be unseemly. Hamilton resembles the larger and older hive of industry in her thrifty application of skill and capital to widely diversified industrial operations. This has been her distinguishing characteristic for at least a generation. Within that period, manufacturing establishments on a scale and with equipments in keeping with the latest demands for cheap and efficient productions, have successively sprung up within her limits. Her increasing workshops have steadily added to her population and enhanced her wealth. Scarcely an important branch of industry is left altogether unrepresented. A statement of the industrial progress of Hamilton, shows that the total capital invested in manufacturing industries in this city, was $8,120,000. The number of employes 14,000, the total amount of wages paid last year was $3,203,500. The total value of the products in the year was $13,980,000. The value of the products per head of population has increased twenty-five per cent. in the ten years.

Hamilton—Eastern View from Mountain

James Street. North

Her factories, equipped with modern machinery and the latest labor-saving devices to minimize the cost of production maintain a daily output of innumerable articles of the metal, wood, and leather industries, of textile fabrics and of glass-ware, pottery, clothing, &c. The curing and packing of meats, and canning of fruits and vegetables are also carried on in accordance with advantageous methods peculiar to the western side of the Atlantic.

Hamilton is distant 40 miles from Toronto; St. Catharines, 31; London, 75; Detroit, 186; Kingston, 200; Montreal, 373; Quebec, 538; Niagara Falls, 42; and Buffalo, 60.

Hamilton and Barton Incline Railroad.

Lighthouse and Drawbridge

CHURCHES AND RELIGIOUS BODIES.

Hamilton is the See city of the Diocese of Niagara (Church of England), and of the Diocese of Hamilton (Roman Catholic). There are in the city 8 Anglican churches, viz.: Christ Church Cathedral, Church of the Ascension, St. Thomas' Church, All Saints', St. Mark's, St. Luke's, St. Matthew's and St. Peter's.

The Roman Catholics have 4 churches, St. Mary's, which is the Cathedral Church, St. Patrick's, St. Lawrence, and one smaller church known as St. Joseph's Church, used chiefly by Germans.

The Presbyterians number 6 churches, designated the Central Church, McNab Street Church, St. Paul's, Knox Church, St. John's and Erskine Church.

Station Grand Trunk Railroad.

On the Beach.

The Methodists have 9 churches, called the Centenary, Wesley, First Methodist, Zion Tabernacle, Simcoe Street, Gore Street, Emerald Street, and the American Methodist Episcopal Churches.

The Baptists have one large and handsome stone church in the centre of the city, with a Mission Church in a remote portion of it. There is also a Baptist church for colored people.

Besides the above religious bodies there is a Congregational Church, a Reformed Episcopal, Brethren of the One Faith, Believers, Evangelical Lutheran, Unitarian, Plymouth Brethren and Salvation Army.

There are also in Hamilton a Jewish Synagogue, a branch of the British and Foreign Bible Society, a Young Men's Christian Association and a Young Women's Christian Association.

King Street, East from James.

Many of the churches of the city are commodious buildings, chiefly of stone and brick, and more or less ornamental in design. The churches are all, in their own way, active in promoting the spiritual welfare of the community. The efforts of all are zealously directed to imparting religious instruction in Sunday Schools, all of which are in a flourishing condition.

SCHOOLS AND EDUCATIONAL INTERESTS.

The School system of the City of Hamilton comprises the Public schools and the Collegiate Institute, together with a Model School and a Training College for teachers.

In the Public schools the course of study, beginning with the kindergarten, comprises reading, writing, English grammar, composition, English literature, history, geography and arithmetic.

In the Collegiate Institute, which pupils enter at the age of about 14 years after having completed the Public school course of study, preparation may be had for entering the Universities, the Medical Schools, the Law Schools, &c.

In the public schools there is an average attendance of 7,359 pupils and more than 200 teachers, and in the Collegiate Institute and Training College there is a yearly attendance of between 500 and 600 students, presided over by a staff of about 30 masters and teachers.

The schools are managed by a Board of Education consisting of twenty members, fourteen of whom are elected by the people and six appointed by the Board of Aldermen.

In the Public schools each pupil is required to pay from one to two dollars a year, in return for which the School Board furnishes him with all the books, stationery, etc., required throughout his course. No charge is made for tuition.

The teachers employed in the different charitable institutions of the city are appointed and paid by the School Board.

In addition to the above Public schools, there are also five separate Roman Catholic Schools in Hamilton. The average number of pupils attending these schools is 1,890. A Ladies' School of high grade is also conducted by that denomination, and is held in high esteem.

The Gore Park.

Court House.

The Wesleyan Methodists also control a Ladies' College in Hamilton, devoted to the higher branches of education for young women. It has been in existence several years and attracts pupils from various parts of Canada.

Besides the Public schools of the city, there are private institutions for commercial and business training, and for art tuition a Public Art School was founded in 1885, and to-day occupies premises which for their equipment are scarcely surpassed by any art school on the American Continent. It is governed by a Board of Directors who are elected annually in September. For the years 1891-1892 the number of males attending the School was 100 and females 90 or a total of 190 students in all.

THE HAMILTON ASSOCIATION is an incorporated Society, organized in 1857, for the cultivation of Science, Literature and Art, the formation of a Museum, Library and Art Gallery, and the illustration of the Physical Characteristics, Natural History and Antiquities of the Country. There are about 200 members, who hold meetings every month from November to May inclusive. Special meetings may be called at any time by the President or on the requisition of any 3 members for the transaction of any stated business. During the existence of the Association numerous papers relating to the fauna, flora and rock conformation of the country surrounding Hamilton have been published under its auspices.

On Bay Front

The Market.

BOARD OF TRADE.

In the year 1845 a Board of Trade was established in Hamilton. That body, from its inception, has exercised a salutary influence over the mercantile affairs of the city, and has been on the alert to promote the construction of railways, canals and other works for opening up the resources and trade of the country. The list of Hamilton merchants is an interesting, if not a long one. Several stand in the front ranks of Canadian trade, and some have won more than a Canadian reputation for their public spirit. If personal references were admissible here, an account of the early merchants of the city and their experiences would be an instructive story.

The Reservoir.

The City Hospital

THE CHARITABLE INSTITUTIONS OF HAMILTON.

Foremost amongst these are the National and Benevolent Societies. They are the St. George's, St. Andrew's, Caledonia, Irish Protestant, Catholic Mutual Benefit, and several associations. These societies seek out and relieve cases of necessity and affliction. They render good service to the community, and receive corresponding appreciation and support. The other charitable institutions comprise a Boys' Home, a Girls' Home, a Home for Aged Women, a Home for the Friendless, an Orphan Asylum, a House of Refuge, and the St. Mary's Orphan Asylum. These have suitable commodious buildings, the outcome of private benevolence, and are sustained by voluntary contributions.

The St. Mary's Asylum is in charge of Sisters of Charity, and the other homes are under the direct management of committees of ladies. The inmates of these homes are well cared for, and the children educated and instructed in the way to make for themselves a respectable living. Donations of all kinds are received by the different charities including money, flour, meal, meat, vegetables and clothing. At Christmas luxuries are not lacking for festive cheer. The average number of inmates in the different homes is: Boys' Home, 90 boys, aged from 5 to 14 years; Girls' Home, 75 girls, aged from 4 to 14 years; St. Mary's Orphan Asylum, 80 girls; Aged Women's Home, 24; House of Providence, about 100 boys and a like number of aged men and women.

Hamilton possesses a magnificent and well equipped Hospital for the sick and injured. It was built a few years ago at a cost to the city of $53,685 and can accommodate 150 patients. The Pavilion style of construction was adopted, with approved methods of obtaining a copious supply of light and air. Last year 734 patients were admitted to the house, and 1083 received treatment as out-patients. It is sustained by the city aided by an annual grant from the Provincial Government, and by contributions from such patients as can afford to pay for maintenance. Last year the Government grant was $7,554.78 and the amount received from patients was $2,760.11; other receipts amounted to $3875, while the expenditure amounted to $21,078.58 leaving a balance of $10,724.94 which was made good by the city. The management of the institution is under the direction of an Hospital Committee appointed yearly by the City Council. Besides a resident medical officer gratuitous attendance is rendered by the medical practitioners of the city.

HAMILTON PUBLIC LIBRARY.

The City of Hamilton possesses about the finest Public library in the Dominion. Located in a magnificent building, centrally situated and open to all, it is one of the chief features of interest in the city. The total number of volumes in the Library at present is 16,515 and new books are continually being added. The Library is divided into four departments: the Circulation department, General Reading Room and Ladies' Reading Room. Books lent for home use last year amounted to 136,904 volumes with a percentage of 54 of works of Fiction; books given for Reference use, 61,200. The number of borrowers' cards is now about 7,250. The number of papers and periodicals on file in the Reading Rooms is 175. It is estimated that over 260,000 visitors used the library last year.

The Royal Hamilton Yacht Club.

CANADA.

ONE of Canada's prominent financiers recently said in a speech: "We are a thoughtful, self-reliant people, as it becomes all Northern races to be, instead therefore, of viewing with envy the instances of rapid money-making in the United States, many in number, it is true, but few in percentage to the toiling millions in that country who may never hope for the comfort which is general in Ontario. Let us then look steadily at our own country and do what we can, as we have in the past, to increase our moderate but quite sufficient prosperity. Few people have shown in the past more enterprise in proportion to population than Canada."

The Dominion of Canada has an area of 3,315,647 square miles, or including its water surface 3,456,383, it is about 3,500 miles from east to west, and 1,400 from north to south. The principal physical features are the Rocky Mountains and the Lawrentian range, the plains of the Northwest Territories and the great Lakes. These lakes, which are five in number, and are remarkable for their size, form a complete system of navigation from the head of Lake Superior to the Atlantic Ocean, a distance of 2,384 miles. Lake Superior is connected with Lake Huron by the Ste. Marie River and the Sault Ste. Marie Canal. Lake Huron flows into Lake St. Clair by the St. Clair River and Lake St. Clair into Lake Erie by the Detroit River. Lake Erie flows into Lake Ontario by the Niagara River, fourteen miles from the mouth of which are the renowned Niagara Falls, 160 feet in height. The Welland Canal connects the two lakes for navigation purposes, and the St. Lawrence River flowing out of Lake Ontario and into the Gulf of St. Lawrence completes this system.

The vast agricultural and mineral resources of Canada are as yet in an embryonic state of development. Between the northern boundary of Ontario and the Rocky Mountains lie the Province of Manitoba and the southern part of the Northwest Territories. This great tract of land is divided into three plateaus, running generally northwest and southeast. The first is known as the Red River valley and Lake Winnipeg plateau and lies entirely in the Province of Manitoba; it is estimated to contain about 7,000 square miles of the best wheat growing land on the Continent or the world. The second plateau has an average altitude of 1,600 feet, and an area of 105,000 square miles. This section is especially favorable for settlement and includes the Assiniboine and Qu'Appelle districts. The third plateau begins on the boundary

Burlington Beach Bay Side

line at the 104th meridian and extends west for 405 miles to the foot of the Rocky Mountains. Its average elevation is about 3,000 feet. Generally speaking the first two are the most favorable for agriculture and the third for grazing. Settlement is proceeding in the first two plateaux at a very rapid rate and is beginning in the third, numerous and prosperous cattle ranches and homesteads having already been established. The northern part of the centre of the Dominion, extending from the Rocky Mountains to Hudson's Bay, has generally been considered as useful only as a preserve for fur bearing animals, but an investigation by a Committee of the Senate in 1888 has upset this idea altogether. The area inquired into was 1,260,000 square miles, and out of this it was estimated 860,000 square miles were fit for settlement and 400,000 square miles useless for cultivation. 656,000 square miles were suitable for potatoes, 407,000 for barley and 316,000 for wheat.

The year 1891 was a particularly good one throughout the Dominion from an agricultural point of view; the total wheat crop was 61,592,822 bushels, of which the Province of Ontario yielded 32,584,026 bushels; all other cereals were rather over the average and the root crops were excellent.

The financial condition of Canada is good as shown by the fact of the Dominion Government having successfully floated a 3 per cent. loan for £2,250,000 ($10,950,000), repayable in 46 years, in London during June, this year, 1892. The minimum price fixed was £91 per cent. and the average price realized was £92.01½. The sum was subscribed for nearly four times over, 420 applications being made representing upwards of £7,000,000. The price obtained was lower than on the previous occasion of borrowing, but such was to be expected when the greatly altered conditions of the market are taken into account. If it had not been that the credit of the Dominion stands remarkably high in the London market the reduction in price would undoubtedly have been much greater. The Revenue for the year 1891 was $38,579,311, showing a surplus of $2,235,743 over expenditure. The total value of Imports in 1891 was $119,967,638, of which $113,345,124 was for home consumption; and the total exports $98,417,296, of which $88,801,066 represented produce of Canada.

Minerals of almost every kind are known to exist in Canada, and their development in future will constitute one of the chief sources of wealth to the country

The Pier.

Gold, silver, copper, nickel, platinum, antimony, asbestos, coal, gypsum, lead, petroleum, etc., are among the chief minerals which have been touched though only in a small way up to the present time. Gold has been found extensively, and paying mines exist in localities extending through 10 degrees of latitude. The value of gold produced in 1890 was $1,149,776 and silver $495,600.

Coal mining will, in the near future, be one of the most important industries in the country; at present the chief sources of supply are Nova Scotia and British Columbia, but in the Northwest Territories and Manitoba it is estimated there are 65,000 square miles of coal bearing strata, and the quantity of fuel known to underlie some portions of this area is estimated at from 4,500,000 to 9,000,000 tons per square mile. This coal varies from lignite to bituminous coal and in the Rocky Mountains large deposits of anthracite have been found, beds of which are now being worked. The importance of, from an Imperial point of view, of having large deposits of smokeless coal within two days' journey of the principal naval stations on the Pacific coast can hardly be overestimated. The amount of coal raised in Canada in 1891 was 3,500,000 tons.

Iron ore is to be found in great abundance and variety in all the provinces of the Dominion, except Manitoba, particularly in Nova Scotia and Ontario; but owing, presumably, both to lack of enterprise and capital it has nowhere been mined to any great extent. Even in Nova Scotia which possesses ore of extreme purity, and which is the only province in the Dominion where flux, fuel and ore are to be found in close proximity. The production is practically limited to the Acadia Mines at Londonderry. In 1891 there were five furnaces in blast and three more in course of construction. There are also twelve rolling mills and steel works in Canada, viz: three in Novia Scotia, two in New Brunswick, four in Quebec, all at Montreal, and three in Ontario. Copper is also present in large quantities in Ontario particularly. Hitherto all the ores have been exported for treatment abroad but smelting works have now been established at Sudbury, Ontario, in which neighborhood what are perhaps the largest deposits of copper in the world have been discovered. The production in 1890 was 6,013,671 lbs. of fine copper, valued at $902,050 and the value of the copper exported amounted to $398,497. There are indications that the output will soon be materially increased, the copper is there and considerable capital has lately been attracted to its development.

The Post Office.

Entrance to Dundern.

In 1883 the first discovery of a deposit of nickeliferous pyrrhotitic was made in the vicinity of Sudbury, Ontario, and since then twenty other deposits have been discovered, and there is no doubt that this ore is present in large quantities. The ore which contains on an average about 2¼ per cent. of nickel, is roasted and smelted into a copper nickel matte, the usual composition of which from average analysis, is about as follows:—copper, 26.91 ; nickel, 14.14 ; iron, 31.335 ; sulphur, 26.95 ; and cobalt, 935. The matte is also said to contain some ounces of platinum to the ton. The amount of fine nickel in the matte produced at and shipped from the Sudbury mines in 1890 was 1,435,742 pounds, which at 65 cents a pound, was worth $933,232. The world's consumption of nickel has been estimated at 800 tons, and previous to these discoveries, the supply came almost entirely from New Caledonia. The consumption of nickel is likely to be very considerably increased by the use of it in alloy with steel to increase the strength and quality of the latter. Experiments which have proved eminently successful have been made in

France and Germany, and also at Annapolis, U. S., more particularly with reference to the use of nickel steel for cannon and armour plate. It has been proved that the elasticity and tensile strength of nickel steel were almost double the limits reached by the best grades of boiler plate steel, and the new metal seems likely to be used, not only for armour plate but for hulls and engines of ships, and indeed for all purposes where a high grade of steel is now used. As a result of the experiments, the United States Government have decided to make use of nickel steel armour plates, and the contract for their manufacture has been awarded, so that the prospects for this new industry round Sudbury are very promising.

Petroleum has been found in Quebec, Nova Scotia, New Brunswick and particularly in the North-west Territories, where it seems certain there is an immense unexplored oil region, but it is in the county of Lambton, Ontario, whence most of the oil has been and is obtained. Oil Springs and Petrolea, being the largest oil-producing districts, the oil being obtained at a depth of from 370 to 500 feet. The first flowing

Dundern.

King Street East from James Street.

well was struck on the 19th of February, 1862 and before October in the same year, there were no less than 35 flowing wells. As there was no accommodation for the storage of this enormous flow, there was a frightful waste, and it is calculated by one authority that between the dates mentioned no less than five million barrels floated off on the waters of an adjoining creek. The annual output for some years has been about 600,000 barrels.

The principal drawbacks to mining developments hitherto have been want of capital, and the fact that a number of the enterprises that have been started have been purely of a speculative character, which has thrown suspicion on genuine undertakings and driven investors to place their funds elsewhere; but as the explorations of the Government Geological Survey are making better known the extent and locality of minerals, and the fiscal policy of the Government is calculated to stimulate production, public attention is becoming more attracted to our mining resources. A large number of members of the British Iron and Steel Association visited the United States in the Autumn of 1890, and many of them inspected the copper and nickel mines of Sudbury, and expressed themselves as being astonished at the evidence of great mineral wealth they met with. It is hoped that as a means of calling attention to the mineral resources of this country their visit will have a beneficial effect.

With regard to the climate of Canada there is probably more misconception generally than about that of any other known country. The idea still prevalent in Europe and elsewhere is that the land is one of perpetual winter and usually covered with snow. In reality the climate is dry, healthy and invigorating. Extending, as the Dominion does, over 20 degrees of latitude, or, from the latitude of Constantinople to the North Pole it has necessarily a wide range of temperature, the extreme dryness of the atmosphere, however, make both cold and heat less actually felt than the readings of the thermometer would lead people to expect. In the maritime provinces the climate resembles that of the British Isles. In Ontario, Quebec and Manitoba the summers are warm and the winters cold, but the cold is pleasant and bracing, and the snow that generally covers the ground is of the greatest benefit alike to the farmer, lumberman and merchant. In the Northwest Territories cattle graze at large throughout the winter, and on the Pacific slope it is very mild and considered by the inhabitants unsurpassed in the world. Instead of the perpetual winter so much talked about the fact is the average winter barely lasts 4½ months and the climate on the whole is the finest in the universe.

Residence of Sir James Turner.

HAMILTON.

As seen by Isabel, Countess of Aberdeen.—She is enchanted with the place, and pays high tribute to the ambitious citizens.

("Through Canada with a Kodak." By Lady Aberdeen, in "*Onward and Upward*."

I am sure that any of you who have travelled will agree that one of its chief pleasures is coming home again. And we felt almost like getting home when we walked into the cool, comfortable dining-room, where breakfast had been prepared for us by those of our household who had preceded us to "Highfield," the house which was to be our home whilst in Canada. Here is a picture of Highfield. I will not give you one of Hamilton, for it is a place which photographs do not do full justice to. The town lies on a gentle rising slope round the head of a beautiful bay, and nestles under a steep ridge, which stretches miles and miles away to the heights of Niagara. Here it shelteringly protects the town, which fondly acknowledges its sway, and which demands from all strangers and newcomers a due tribute of loyal admiration for the mountain. As an illustration of this admiration, the day after we arrived a boy, of about thirteen, came up to Lord Aberdeen as he was walking in the grounds and said: "Is Lord Haddo at home?" "Well, no, he is not, but I am his father. What do you want with him?"

"Well, I want to interview him, and ask what his Lordship thought of our city, and I wanted to put the interview in my father's newspaper."

Lord Aberdeen was rather startled in spite of having become somewhat familiarized to the custom of "interviewing" which prevails universally on the other side of the water, by means of which public men make known their views. He had scarcely, however, expected his eleven-year-old son to be called upon to give his opinions as yet, and he tried to explain to the youthful journalist that in the Old Country boys were not expected to air their views so soon. But our young friend was not so easily baffled. He still persisted in asking "If Lord Haddo had made arrangements to inspect the public buildings of the city, and especially if he had visited the "mountain," and what he thought of that. Lord Aberdeen informed him that his boy was at that moment enjoying a clamber up the steep, and did his best to satisfy his enterprising enquirer by expressing his own appreciation of the heights under whose shade they were standing.

Well, climb up this mountain (almost on the side of which stands Highfield), in the cool of an early September evening, and see the town spreading itself out east and west before you, wide and well kept streets, trim lawns as green as those in England, houses nestling amongst trees, handsome buildings, church spires and factory chimneys competing for pre-eminence. And beyond the city, and its manufactories, and its wharves, lies the bay, all gleaming with the bright colors of the setting sun, amid which little yachts and pleasure boats are making their way home. Our thoughts linger fondly over the restful days spent in this peaceful retreat, and I fancy that both we and our children associate Highfield to a great extent with sunshine and butterflies. Perhaps we had a little more of the former than we cared for just at first—for days with the thermometer over 90 degrees in the shade do not as a rule recommend themselves to Scotish-bred folk. But after all we had not much to grumble at, for the heat was not accompanied by our much-dreaded foes, the blood-thirsty mosquitoes. True, this race of pests, who are supposed to avoid Hamilton as a rule, had sent out this year an advance guard to survey the place, and even we, though late in the season, heard ominous trumpetings as we laid our heads on the pillows, but it seemed that as yet they were but vegetarian specimens of the race who had arrived, for none of our party suffered at their hands. Nor did they suffer at ours. We did not capture a single specimen. And this is a great thing to say for such an insect-hunting family as we must confess ourselves to be.

As we sat in the pretty secluded grounds which surround Highfield that first day, we became conscious that we were by no means alone, and our children who had joined us, were soon in full pursuit of the wonderful creatures which looked like butterflies on the wing, but turned into grasshoppers when they alighted, of the "Camberwell beauties," and the "Admirals," and the many other bright-colored visitors of our garden. But we did not do much that first day—we had not the necessary implements, and we had to sally forth in search of the wherewithal to make butterfly nets, and killing-boxes and specimen boxes, and I know not what. And here let me introduce the four young butterfly-hunters of Highfield. Of course, if you ever hear that their mother, your staid editor, joined them in their wild pursuit of her majesty, the glorious red-winged, swift-flying "Queen of Spain," or if you hear of her anointing telegraph poles and trees with honey and molasses, and flitting about with others of the staff of "*Onward and Upward*," at dead of night, with lanterns capturing the unwary but magnificent moths, who had imbibed the sweet draughts too freely, you will surely not believe such tales.

Suffice it to say that a really beautiful collection of moths and butterflies resulted from our stay at Highfield, a collection doomed to an untimely end, for during their transit home, they got so battered that it was only left to the two editors to mingle their tears together over their ashes. We must not ask you to linger with us in our lamentations over our broken treasures. We live in hope of replacing them some day, and meanwhile we have other memories of Hamilton which we wish to share with you.

A hundred years ago Hamilton had barely begun to exist. But the few who were then plowing up the land on which the city now stands, were of the stamp which makes nations to rejoice over her children. You will remember that after the war which resulted in the independence of the United States, a number of American people who had remained true to the British flag throughout the war, resolved to give up their lands and their homes and migrate to Canada, rather than dwell in a land which had revolted from the Crown to which they were so loyal. Canada right joyfully held out her arms to these noble-hearted refugees.

Ontario was then unpeopled, and so 200 acres of land in this rich Province were granted free to every one of those United Empire Loyalists, as they were called. U. E. Loyalists they are called now for short, and those who can trace their parentage to these families count it a proud descent and glory in it.

One of the earliest of these refugees was Robert Land, and he selected the head of the lake, more because of the game to be found there and the scenery, than because of the fertility of the soil. His first acre was ploughed with a hoe, sown with a bushel of wheat, and harrowed with a leafy bough. He was his own miller, too, for some years until a French-Canadian arrived and set up a mill some seven miles away. Then other farmers came, and in 1813, George Hamilton laid out his farm in village lots, and gave the future town its name. Lying, as it does, so near the frontier, it did not escape anxious times during the war of 1812 and the following years, and in 1832 it narrowly escaped destruction at the hands of a terrible visitation of the cholera, and the same year by a raging fire. These trials did but prove the mettle of the inhabitants of the young town, and perhaps furnish the reason why its streets are now so broad, and so cared for, its buildings so solid, its sanitary arrangements so thoroughly looked into, its provisions against fire so complete. A popular writer described Hamilton in 1858 as "the ambitious and stirring little city," and the name stuck; only "little" she is no longer, being the third city in the Dominion, having a population of over 50,000, and her enviers have missed out the "stirring," so if you seek for news of Hamilton in the general newspaper, you must look for it under the heading "The Ambitious City." But she is not, and need not, be ashamed of the nickname, for she has shown herself ambitious to some purpose. I could take up a large part of these Canadian gossips by describing to you the public buildings and their uses, the magnificent school buildings, and the good work that goes on in them, the institutions, social, literary, philanthropic and religious—the many manufactories which cause Hamilton to be regarded as the Birmingham of Canada, the acres of vineyards around, the fruit gardens and orchards, which give this part of the country the name of "The garden of Canada;" the churches of all denominations whose services we attended, and above all the people of Hamilton. But having regard to the length and purport of these sketches, I will not launch into so large a subject. Suffice it to say that the kindness and good fellowship extended to us by the inhabitants of Hamilton, of all classes, did what only true, hearty courtesy and kindness can do, viz.: we felt ourselves to be no mere tourists and strangers, but fellow citizens of "no mean city." And in proof of this assertion, I have by my side here, in the office of "*Onward and Upward*," two beautifully bound books concerning the birds and plants of Canada, and which were presented to me by the Free Library committee, as being the first citizen to apply for a book on the occasion of Lord Aberdeen's opening of the new building. (I must confide to you, however, that your president's character had to be inquired into before I was admitted as a reader. I had to produce a certificate of honesty, and so forth, signed by two citizens of Hamilton. You will be glad to know that I found two senators willing to vouch for me.)

There is no doubt that if you want really to know something of a country, its customs, and its people, it is a great advantage if you can settle down in some typical place for a few weeks, instead of merely travelling through and seeing the sights of each town. In the latter way you may see more, perhaps, of the buildings, institutions, &c., for, if you have but a day or two, you can map out your time, and spend it in driving from one place to another, and you thus get through a good deal; but if you make yourself at home anywhere for a bit you will not do the tourist so much, but if you mix at all with the people you almost unconsciously get to understand them and their ways of thinking, and the whys and wherefores of their customs and institutions. This was an experience, living our every-day life, interchanging visits, reading the daily papers of all sections of politics, mingling with clergy, statesmen, merchants, agriculturists, &c., and hearing various opinions from all sorts and conditions of men. And the sum total of what we learnt made us feel that the more the Old Country learnt to know her grown-up child over the sea, the more she would be proud of her in all ways, and the more earnestly did it make us wish and pray that the future of Canada may be worthy of her past and that the present God-fearing, industrious, simple, education-loving stock may only be reinforced by those worthy to combine with them in building up a grand country and nation.

As I have said before, none need fear to go out to Canada who are ready to work. Our lads and lasses who went out with us with the intention of settling (and of whom I gave you a group sitting outside Highfield), have nearly all found happy homes. One, indeed, has come back because of her father's death, but I feel much tempted to give you extracts from some of the letters of others. They have not suffered at all from the cold of the winter, but seem to have enjoyed the merry winter customs, and seeing all the skating and the sleighing going on round about them. For one thing heartiness of Canadians towards newcomers counts for a great deal: they do all they can to make everyone feel welcome, and one of them—there is a freeness, a sense of equality, a consciousness that everyone will be taken just for what he or she is worth, and nothing more or less, which cannot altogether be attained in the Old World, and which must always be refreshing to anyone of independent spirit. "Prove yourself to be a man, a woman, and we shall respect you, and you shall have an equal chance with any of us, and what is more we will do our best to put you into the running with us from the first." Human nature is undoubtedly the same everywhere, and Canadians would not wish to claim for themselves immunity from all faults, but they may fairly claim that anyone wishing to live a free, independent, self respecting, law abiding and God-fearing life has few impediments under the government the public life and customs, the bright climate, and the sanguine temperament of Canada and her folk as they will find in any land under the sun.

Lord Aberdeen was accused of distributing what was termed "taffy to the Dominion" (is this word derived from "toffee" I wonder? Anyway it means something sweet,) in some of his speeches in Canada. Perhaps I shall be accused of following in his footsteps. Well, we can only speak of that we do know, and that we have seen, and I can honestly say that I am not conscious of having flattered. Next month I invite you to accompany us to some of Canada's autumn fairs.

Mountain Avenue Road—Hamilton.

For the benefit of the thousands of strangers who will visit the city, going to or coming from the World's Fair, a special committee has been appointed by the City Council who will lay out plans so that every information may be promptly obtained by the visitor concerning matters pertaining to the manufacturing industries, commercial advantages, drives, scenery, accommodations, etc.

We wish that space could be found in this souvenir for a short sketch of every one of the vast establishments centered in Hamilton. We can only, however, select a few of each branch, so the reader may judge of the trade and commerce done, and the kind of people we have amongst us, who are doing it.

Bank of British North America.

The oldest existing Bank in Hamilton, is the Bank of British North America. It is situated on the south side of King Street, a substantial stone structure owned by the Bank. It is three stories high, of modern architectural design. The Bank of British North America is an English institution, with the head office in London, but nearly all its business is done in Canada. Its capital is a million pounds sterling. Being a British Bank and firmly established with abundant capital, it has been a bulwark of strength to many of our industries in the day of financial struggle. The Bank does business from the Atlantic to the Pacific, and its New York business is very extensive, and it issues bills of exchange and letters of credit upon all parts of the world.

Elsinore.

This is a Summer Sanitarium for sick children, and is a monument to the generosity of the Hon. W. E. and Mrs. Sanford, who at their own cost, constructed the building and then handed it over to the authorities of the Infants' Home.

It is situated on Hamilton Beach, near to Church Crossing Station, and commands an extensive view of both lake and bay. No finer location could have been well selected for such an institution.

The Jail.

The building is of beautiful design, rising to a height of three stories and surrounded on all sides by spacious covered verandahs where the children can enjoy to the full, the health giving breezes of the lake

Ample grounds about the building, also afford a playground for the little ones.

Not only is the exterior beautiful to look upon, but the interior is complete in every respect; the rooms are lofty, airy and well lighted; pictures adorn the walls, and amusements for the children abound. Many little ones have been benefited by a stay here during the sultry summer months, and it is safe to say that numbers are now alive and well, who, but for the health-giving opportunity afforded by this noble gift of Senator Sanford, would, to-day, be filling premature and untimely graves.

CANADA LIFE ASSURANCE COMPANY.

Amongst the many magnificent buildings in Hamilton, that of the Canada Life Assurance Company occupies the first rank; and as an Assurance Company it is second to none. Organized in 1847, in Hamilton, where its head offices are situated, it has established branches throughout the Dominion; it has also agencies in London, England, and Detroit, Michigan. U. S.

The Capital of the Canada Life Assurance Company now amounts to over $13,000,000 while it has an annual income of nearly a quarter of a million dollars. The new assurances applied for last year were 2,507 in number and aggregated close on $6,000,000 in amount, of these 2,107 policies were granted and the sum assured was $5,255,021 with a semi-annual premium income of $178,191,00. At the close of the year 1891, the total assurances in force amounted to $56,218,318 which certainly tends to demonstrate the confidence the public have in this company. Its income is now double what it was ten years ago, and to successfully handle an income of $7,000 dollars a day demonstrates far more forcibly the ability of the management, than could be shown by a page of printed matter. There is no more popular assurance Corporation in the whole of the Dominion, and assuredly none in whom the public place such implicit confidence as the Canada Life Assurance Company.

The management of this great and successful institution is governed by the following well known gentlemen in Canada: A. G. Ramsay, Esq., President; R. Hill, Esq., Secretary; W. T. Ramsey, Esq., Superintendent.

BOARD OF DIRECTORS:

F. WOLFERSTAN THOMAS, Esq., Montreal,
The Very Rev. G. M. INNES, Dean of Huron London,
F. W. GATES, Esq., Hamilton, Vice-President,
The Hon. Mr. JUSTICE BURTON, Toronto,
N. MERRITT, Esq., Toronto,
JOHN STUART, Esq., Hamilton,

ADAM BROWN, Esq., Hamilton,
WILLIAM HENDRIE, Esq., Hamilton,
Lieut.-Governor Hon. GEO. A. KIRKPATRICK, Toronto,
A. G. RAMSAY, Esq., Hamilton, President,
A. ALLAN, Esq., (H. & A. ALLAN) Montreal,
GEORGE A. COX, Esq., Toronto,

Col. Sir. CASIMIR S. GZOWSKI, K.C.M.G., A.D.C. to the Queen, Toronto.

MEDICAL ADVISERS:

J. D. MACDONALD, M. D.,   J. A. MULLIN, M. D.

GENERAL AGENTS:

H. M. POUSSETT,   DR. D. LOWREY,   H. E. GATES,   T. A. GALE.
D. KIDD, Hamilton District Agent.

Canada Life Assurance Co. Building.

The Hamilton Club

JAMES TURNER COMPANY, Wholesale Grocers and Wine Merchants, Hamilton, Ontario.

The work professing to give an outline of Hamilton's industries and chief business houses would be incomplete without giving prominence to the above old firm which was started over forty years ago, and from that day to this they have enjoyed the proud position of being the leading wholesale grocery house in Ontario.

The present members of the firm are Alexander Turner, Lloyd T. Mawburn and Alex G. Osborne. The senior is a public spirited man and holds the position of director in the Hamilton Provident and Loan Society, chairman of the Board of Education of this city and is also an active member of the Board of Trade, of which he is an ex-president.

James Turner Company initiated the North West business; the late Senator Turner, who was then senior member of the firm, in 1867 went to Fort Garry, Red River Country, via St. Paul, and his great success then laid the corner-stone of the good trade which Hamilton and Ontario now enjoy in that country.

In 1872 they built at Winnipeg, the first brick building in Manitoba or the North West and it is standing there to-day.

The business of this firm extends from the Rockies to the seaboard. Their shipping facilities are so good that they can ship from two to three carloads of mixed goods a day.

They buy in all the first markets of the world, and for this reason the trade who buy from them always do so with a confidence knowing they are getting goods at the right price and that they will be treated fairly and honorably as that is the principle of business the firm adopted when starting, and which they have ever since adhered to, and they are to-day enjoying as large a business as they have ever done despite all opposition.

The Great Central Fair and Industrial Exhibition Association of Hamilton.

For over a quarter of a century the Great Central Fair has been one of the popular institutions of the city, and in the month of September in each year, thousands of people have come here from every corner of the province, to witness a display of horses, cattle, sheep and pigs, agricultural implements, every description manufactured goods, fruits vegetables and flowers, unequaled at any fair held on the continent of America. To keep up its past reputation, and to compete with the immense strides which are being made in all large cities in exhibition attractions, a new company has been formed new and extensive grounds purchased near the city limits, modern buildings erected, and race track—said to be the best in America —laid out. Two railway tracks run into the grounds, and the Electric Railway will carry passengers to its gates.

Under the general management of such a Board of Directors, composed of gentlemen known all over the Dominion, for their energy, enterprize and success with everything they take in hand.

Hamilton has no doubts of a great future for the Association while Messrs. Wm. Hendrie, J. M. Lottridge, F. C. Bruce, Geo. Roach and J. J. Stuart are its leading spirits.

Weslyan Ladies' College

Young Men's Christian Association.

GRAND TRUNK RAILWAY

Hundreds of thousands of people will be carried to the World's Fair by this excellent railway. Thousands from Europe will take care in obtaining their tickets, that they will ask for them via "the old reliable road by way of Niagara Falls and Canada, direct to Chicago, with a lay-off ticket for Hamilton," to brace them up for the turmoil of Chicago's whirl of sight-seeing, if in returning, to recuperate, and give them an idea of Canadian life before going "Eastward, Ho."

The Grand Trunk Railway system of affiliated roads, now represents an aggregate of 4,286 miles. Its capital accounts show an expenditure of over £56,000,000 sterling. It is steel railed throughout and have 18,200 cars and over 1,000 engines. They have their own workshops, foundries and all the modern machinery necessary to the independence of the service.

The Grand Trunk employs an army of about 20,000 men, and the road has always been recognized as the great international route between the Eastern and Western States. At the Niagara frontier interchanging traffic with all trunk lines leading from New York, thence direct by the western frontier of either Windsor to Detroit or Sarnia by tunnel to Port Huron.

The company possesses its own Ocean terminus at Portland, and reaches by its connections all chief American Ports. It will thus be seen that the Grand Trunk Railway is to be regarded as an undertaking of which the Dominion may well be proud, and it has a wide and popular reputation exercising large Influences in the railway councils of the Continent. The extreme limits of the entire system its affiliations and friendly connections, are Halifax, Portland, Boston, New York, Detroit and Chicago.

Hamilton Public Library.

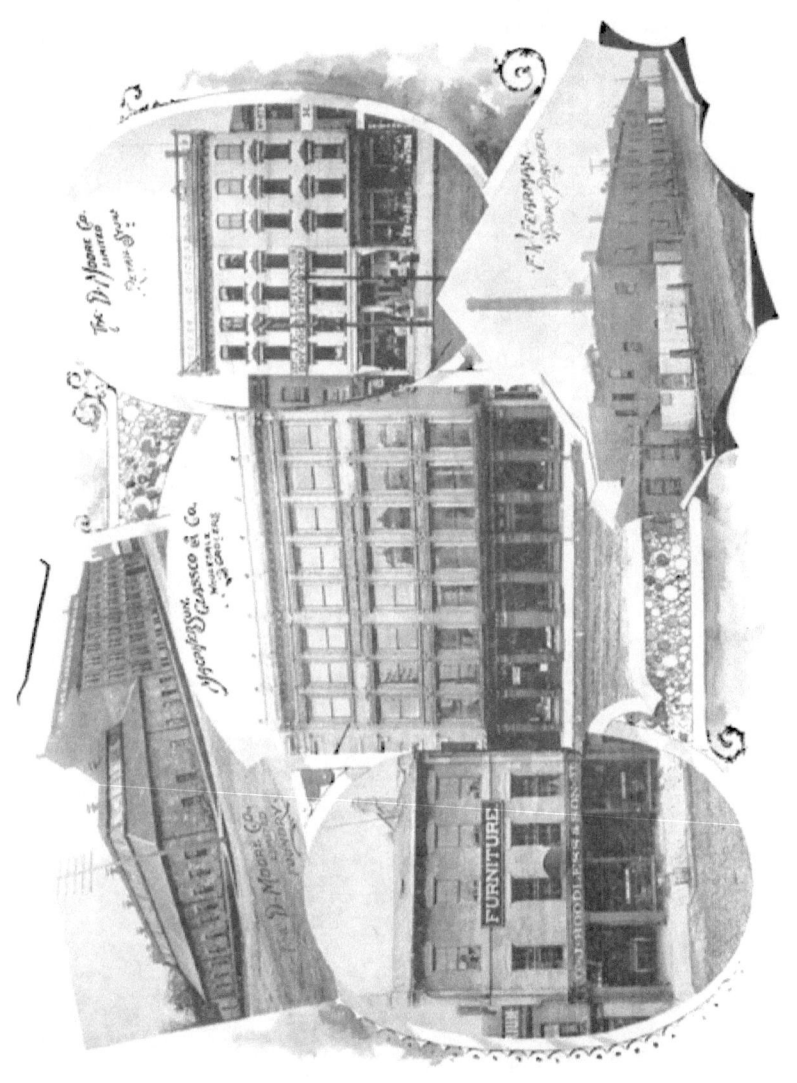

HAMILTON LANDED BANKING AND LOAN COMPANY.

The Landed Banking and Loan Company of Hamilton, whose premises are situated immediately to the rear of the Canada Life Assurance premises, was incorporated in 1876 with a subscribed capital of $700,000. The business of the company is chiefly restricted to Ontario and Manitoba. To its general banking business is added a Savings Bank, at which deposits from one dollar and upwards are received, the current rates of interest being allowed from date of deposit to withdrawal, and also a Loan Department, in which money is lent upon improved farm or city property. In the year 1879, three years after its initiation, the company received and accepted applications for 59 loans, aggregating $59,254.55; the total number of loans in that year, however, were 169, with a total of $222,799 in amount. The deposits showed an increase of $57,949.55, which amounted to $100,099.39 for the year. Out of the profits two half-yearly payments at the rate of eight per cent. per annum were paid. In 1888, the deposits amounted to over half a million, with a reserve fund of $83,000, and in 1891 the deposits were $560,186.41. Reserve fund $118,000 within a fraction of 11 per cent. on the paid-up capital. The total assets at the close of the fiscal year amounted to $1,792,913, showing a rapid and steady progress since the inception of the company in 1879.

Ably directed by Matthew Leggatt, Esq., President, John Waldie, Esq., Vice-President, C. W. Cartwright, Esq., Treasurer, and a most efficient Board of Directors, composed of such gentlemen as Messrs. R. Æ. Kennedy, President of the Times Printing Company, I. Hobson, Chief Engineer of the Grand Trunk Railway, I. I. Mason, Accountant and Grand Secretary A. F. and A. M., H. McLaren and Thomas Bain, M.P., the majority of whom having held office since the commencement of the bank, are thoroughly conversant with the business in all its details. The Landed Banking and Loan Company is fully launched upon the sea of prosperity.

THE CANADIAN PACIFIC RAILWAY COMPANY.

In our Souvenir we have not confined ourselves to Hamilton entirely, and have mentioned many points in connection with Canada in general, but in doing so we cannot omit to mention therewith a railway company, which has by its immense grasp of the future condition of affairs, been able to bring the Dominion before the whole world, as the great grain-growing section of the universe, the most magnificent scenery of America, and the finest climate in existence.

The Canadian Pacific Railway bands with iron, British North America, from extreme east to extreme west from the Atlantic Ocean to the Pacific Ocean—a wonder of the age, for the marvellous speed made in building amid all difficulties and completing this wondrous highway, and opening up an immense new country to the world at large. It goes still further for it continues to connect the iron band with its lines of steel steamers, and thus girths the whole world.

Start from Liverpool, if you will, thence across the Bay of Biscay, and onward to the Mediterranean—Gibraltar being the first port of call—down the Mediterranean to Naples, thence to Port Said, thence Suez, and passing through the Red Sea, across the Indian Ocean to Ceylon, port of call, Colombo. Leaving Colombo, we cross the Bay of Bengal to Penang, the straits of Malacca to Singapore. From Singapore the route lies direct through the China Sea to Hong Kong—the most eastern of British possessions. From Hong Kong to Woosung for Shanghai, thence to Nagaski; after leaving Nagaski, via the Sea of Japan to Kobe, thence to Yokohama. From Yokohama across the Pacific Ocean to Vancouver, British Columbia—one of our own provinces of Canada. We bid farewell to the Canadian Pacific steamships and commence the trans-continental journey across Canada from the Pacific to the Atlantic by the Canadian Pacific Railways, unrivalled and picturesque route through to Mon-

treal, Halifax, Boston or New York, thence onward across the Atlantic to the starting place, Liverpool.

Whether in ships or in railway the C. P. R. R. have done all things well; everything of the latest and best known designs for safety and comfort. Luxurious cars, where the traveller dines and sleeps, bathes, smokes and reads, as in a hotel, he beholds the panorama of the Continent. There is revealed to him every physical feature of the new world; the great lakes, the great rivers, the plains and prairies, forests and swamps, and finally the greatest mountain ranges of the Continent succeed one another in rapidly moving pictures.

This company has built along the route magnificent hotels for the comfort of its passengers, notably at Bariff and Silkirks. If you come from Europe next year don't leave America for your home till you have had a run over the greatest railway in the world, and through the greatest and grandest country on earth. That would be our advice to you, for neither Europe, Asia, Africa or America has such a railway, or such a country as the Canadian Pacific Railway, or our own Canada.

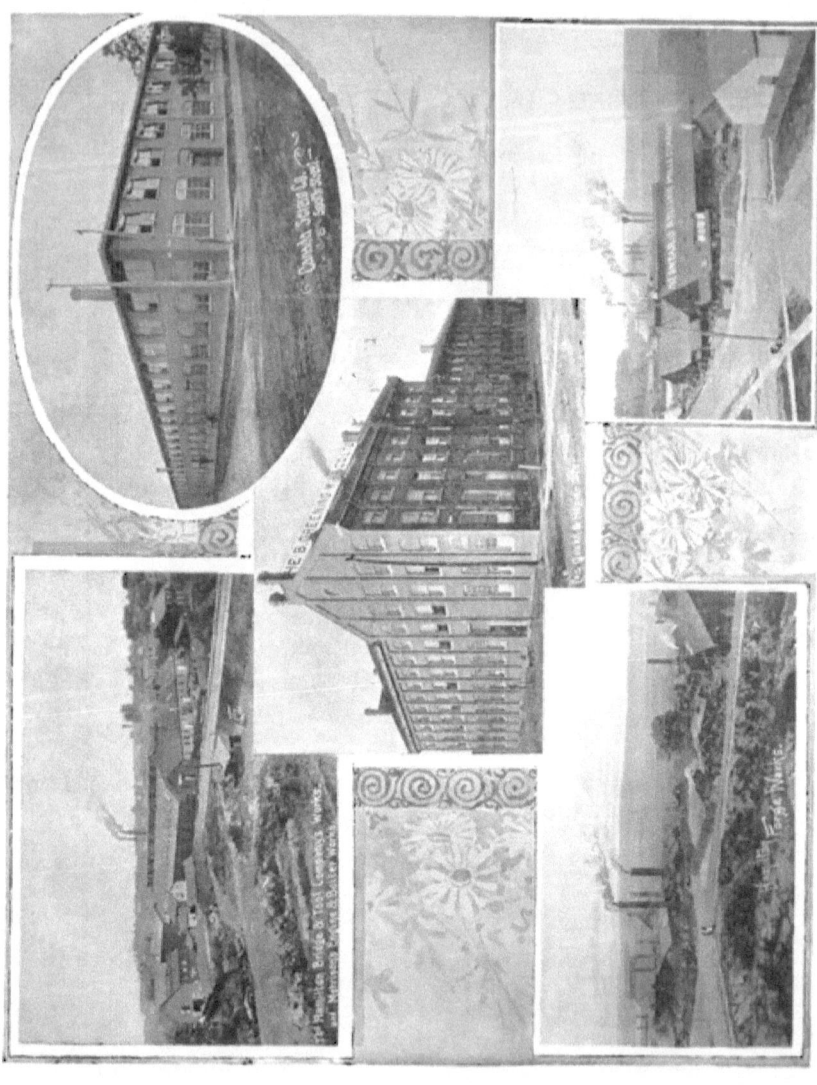

Long & Bisby, Wool Merchants, McNab Street.

Among the largest dealers of wool in Canada or the United States, the firm of Long & Bisby stand foremost. They commenced business in 1867. Their warehouse is a substantial stone building on McNab Street, a little north of the market. Their reputation stands high throughout the whole of British North America—in fact, wherever wool is marketable in any land.

The shipments of wool to the firm are made from every Province in the Dominion, and foreign grades are imported by them for manufacturers in Canada.

The Laidlaw Manufacturing Company.

This firm has established its works at 84, 86, 88, 90 Mary Street, and has one of the finest show rooms in the City. The company manufactures stoves, ranges, enamelled ware, hot air furnaces and castings of every description. The business was first instituted by W. and J. Turnbull over thirty years ago. In 1869 Mr. Laidlaw was taken into the business under the firm name of Turnbull & Co. Five years later Mr. Laidlaw assumed control of the business and the present firm's name was adopted. The company has been very successful in their business, and their line of stoves and ranges. The "Peninsular," is one which has attained an enviable reputation all over the American Continent. The "Boynton" and "Peninsular" hot air furnaces are also manufactured by this company, and have attained a high position among

Royal Hotel.

the trade throughout the Dominion. Two new lines have been added to their list of manu
factures within the past year or two. One of them —the Union Hot water and Steam Radiator —
has had a remarkable sale, and being a standard article, the prospects for its continued
popularity are excellent. The other new line is that of brick and tile machinery and brickmakers'
supplies. The Henry Martin brick machine, made by this firm, is acknowledged the best
machine made, and in its manufacture at this foundry it loses none of its excellence.
Newell's pulverizer, Raymond's perfection re-press, Leader brick and tile machine, and the
Victoria semi-dry press machine, are also included in this line besides all other necessary
machinery in the brick-making line.

VICTORIA WIRE MILLS.

Established 1859. Incorporated 1889. The illustrations herewith will convey a good
idea of the extensive works of the B. Greening Wire Company, limited, of this city, although
the rope department, store rooms and wood-working department in the rear are not shown.
The floor space contained in the various buildings amount to 55,450 square feet, and large
additions are contemplated in the near future. As general manufacturers of wire goods, the
firm is the most extensive in Canada. The principal lines manufactured are wire rope, wire
cloth, perforated sheet metals, bank and office counter railing, wire fencing, metallic lathing,

sofa and chair springs, foundry supplies, wire goods, etc., for which they find a market from the Atlantic to the Pacific. For the convenience of their Eastern customers they have established a branch agency at 422 St. Paul Street, Montreal, where their principal lines are kept in stock. They are also sole wholesale agents in Ontario for the sale of the celebrated Ontario Wire Fencing Company's goods. The present year is the thirty-third anniversary of the establishment of the works in Canada, and sees many important changes and additions in the business. The firm of B. Greening & Co. has been succeeded by B. Greening Wire Company (Limited), the stock, however, being all taken up by the old firm and management. The new wire mill, erected to draw and manufacture all kinds of bright, tinned, galvanized, coppered, iron and steel wire, is now in operation. The company have purchased and now control all the best and most successful patents for fire-proof metallic lathing, an article that will in time entirely supplant the old wooden lath in all good buildings. Arrangements have just been completed with and extensive American firm for the sole right to manufacture in Canada a steel wire chain that is destined to come largely into general use for trace-chains, dog-chains, cow-ties, coil chains, etc. The chain will be placed on the market at a lower price than the imported English or German chains, while the quality is far superior, being more than double the strength. It will thus be seen that this enterprising firm are not relying upon past successes, but are rapidly developing old and new lines, and are, no doubt, destined to become one of the largest industries in this city of manufactures.

Elsinore, Burlington Beach.

Orphan and Aged Women's Home

THOMAS LAWRY & SON.

One of the most extensive of our various industries, and one which within the last few years has made rapid strides towards the height of prosperity, is that of Thos. Lawry & Son, known as the Hamilton Packing House. In 1864 the enterprise was established by Thomas Lawry, since which time the business has steadily increased, until now the industry is the most extensive of its kind in the Dominion.

The excellent quality of the goods turned out is, no doubt, the key to its prosperity, as the L. & S. and Imperial brands of meats and lard have made for themselves a reputation as wide as the Continent, large consignments being made daily to the Maritime provinces, Newfoundland, Manitoba and British Columbia markets, besides producing the principal Ontario supply. Within the last few years the capacity of the Hamilton Packing House has been doubled by extensive improvements, besides which the Argyle and Ontario Packing Houses have also been secured, the latter of which alone having a capacity of 1,000 hogs per day.

The present members of the firm are Thomas Lawry and his son T. H. Lawry.

Sawyer & Massey Company (Limited).

This firm is a combination of two of the most extensive and widely known manufacturers of agricultural implements in the Dominion, and are the successors of the long established firm of L. D. Sawyer & Co., which for the past fifty-three years has been prominently identified with the history of Hamilton, and has held an honored position among her leading industries.

Founded in the year 1836 by the firm of McQuesten & Fisher, it was for some years carried on in a modest looking building on the corner of James and Merrick Streets, the present site of the Royal hotel, but increasing business called for larger premises, the buildings now occupied on Wellington Street north were erected in the year 1854, a year fraught with events of great interest and importance to the rising city of Hamilton, as being that in which the iron horse made his first entry on the newly laid rails of the Great Western Railway.

In addition to the making of agricultural implements, the new factory engaged extensively for a number of years in supplying the railroad with many of the principal castings. In the same year also 1854—Mr. Luther D. Sawyer first became connected with the works, and in 1858, being joined by his brothers, Samuel and Payson, the business passed entirely into their hands, and has since been confined exclusively to the manufacture of agricultural implements, a specialty being now made of threshers and engines.

The Drill Hall.

McPherson's Shoe Factory.

Further changes in the personnel of the firm afterwards took place by the death of Samuel Sawyer, the removal of Payson to the Western States, and the subsequent accession of Henry P. Coburn and Jonathan Ames, who since 1886, till the dissolution of partnership in the year 1889, have taken a leading part in the conduct of the business, and it is not too much to say, that to the progressive enterprise of L. D. Sawyer & Co. is largely due much of the great improvement that has been made of recent years in harvesting and threshing machinery. Mr. Sawyer and Mr. Ames, wishing to retire from active life, disposed of their interests to H. A. Massey & Sons, of Toronto, who saw in the thresher and engine business a branch that would work successfully and harmoniously with their own output of binder, mowers, etc., their thorough and almost world-wide organization giving them unrivalled facilities for putting on every market every kind of machinery required by the agriculturalist.

With Mr. H. P. Coburn as vice-President and Manager of the new firm, his long and varied experience in this line, the capacity and efficiency of the works, and the constantly increasing demand for high class threshing machinery, it is reasonable to assume that the future history of this business will be, if possible, still more brilliant than the past, and it is intended to spare no pains or expense to increase not only its efficiency, but also to add to the present list of machines made, such others as a widening market and the increasing intelligence of Canadian agriculturists may require

The Federal Life Building.

The large works of this firm are situated at the corner of John and Cannon Streets and the busy hum of machinery which is heard in the vicinity, gives evidence of the extent of the business done. The firm commenced business in 1864 and at present employs about two hundred men. Success has marked the career of the business at its inception, and has followed it down to the present time. The output of the establishment is varied and comprises stoves, ranges, hot air furnaces, wagon, carriage, and saddlery hardware, imperial standard scales, oil stoves and miscellaneous goods. Their Jewel hot air furnaces have been a successful line and although a new furnace their manufacture dating back for only two years they are now known through almost the entire Dominion. The "Jewel" stoves and ranges are also manufactured, and the large number of sales give evidence of the high estimation in which they are held by the public. Burrow, Stewart & Milne's imperial standard scales need no wordy praise. Their work speaks their worth, and the manufacturers claim that they are now doing the largest scale business in Canada, and offer as substantiation of the fact, the reports of the government inspector of weights and measures, each scale manufactured being tested and stamped with the government seal by that officer. The "Victory" oil stove is another manufacture of this firm and with its latest improvements is one of the safest, most durable and most economical oil stoves made. Their wagon, carriage and saddlery hardware is of the finest class, and a large trade is done in this line.

THE ROYAL HOTEL.

This well known hotel, the most fashionable and commodius in the city, under its present management and proprietorship of Messrs. Hood & Brother, has been thoroughly refitted and renovated with every regard to comfort and luxury. The reputation of the house, as for first-class genuine comfort extends all over America. It is elegantly furnished throughout, rooms en suite, with bath-rooms, etc., attached on every floor. It is centrally located on one of the principal streets and near to the banks and business houses.

THE ST. NICHOLAS HOTEL.

Situated on James Street, north, not far from the City Hall and market, has recently undergone alterations and improvements to meet the fast increasing trade, and anticipating the travel of 1893 to our city. The proprietor is a model landlord and has the happy knack of making his guests feel at home.

THE AMERICAN HOTEL.

Is a large brick building on King Street, west, not far from the Gore. Its proprietor, F. W. Bearman, is very popular, and having owned the American for many years is well known all over Ontario. The hotel is well furnished, ably conducted, and is cozy and comfortable.

THE DOMINION HOTEL.

Is situated nearly opposite to the American, built of brick, does a good trade, the rooms are comfortable and well furnished. The Dominion has always borne an excellent reputation.

THE COMMERCIAL HOTEL.

Centrally situated at the corner of York and Park Sts., has undergone repairs recently. Mr. Harry Maxey has lately become the proprietor. It is very comfortably furnished, and under his jurisdiction this hotel has become a very popular home resort. Cosey comfort is the order of the day.

THE FRANKLIN HOUSE.

Is on King Street, west, is well conducted in every way. The rooms are good and always clean and neat. Mine Host of the Franklin is always on the alert to make his guests happy.

THE VICTORIA HOTEL.

King Street, east, a good standard hotel, good rooms, every care and attention paid for the comfort of guests, the present proprietor has only recently taken charge. He is a very popular young man, kind and courteous, and will certainly keep up the good reputation the Victoria has always enjoyed.

Residence of Hon W E. Sanford

MESSRS. LUCAS, STEELE AND BRISTOL.

The wholesale grocery trade of Hamilton is one of the strongest features of the business of the city. The many and extensive wholesale houses in the city practically control the trade not only in Ontario, but in Manitoba, the North West Territories and British Columbia. The trade is in the hands of energetic and enterprizing men, who thoroughly understand the business, and no set of men have a more intimate acquaintance and complete understanding of the ramifications of this important trade than the gentlemen composing the firm of Messrs. Lucas, Steele and Bristol.

The firm was establised in 1859 and now occupies a leading place in the wholesale grocery trade of Hamilton. Its extensive premises situated on MacNab Street, north, are solid and substantial, built of stone. Since the foundation of the business it has enjoyed an uninterrupted prosperity to the present day.

For those interested in the conduct of a great commercial enterprise, a visit to their premises will be time well employed. On each spacious floor is a display of well arrayed goods of every variety handled by the trade The firm employ a very large staff of assistants in Hamilton, which has now assumed very large proportions. A business on such a scale as that of Messrs, Lucas & Co., does much towards the prosperity of a city and more especially is this so when the individual members of a firm identify themselves with its affairs. All the heads of the firm are prominent members of the Board of trade. Mr. George E. Bristol being an ex-President of that representative body.

Travellers cover all territory west of Toronto to the Pacific Ocean.

F. W. FEARMAN.

The firm of F. W. Fearman is known throughout the Dominion and elsewhere as about the largest of the many large establishments devoted to the treatment of pork in all its branches. This firm annually receives from the farmer about 50,000 hogs, and furnishing to the retail trade and consumers generally, product in the form of hams, bacon, shoulders, spiced rolls, long clears, mess pork, short cut pork, lard, etc., in matchless quality. Founded in 1852, the firm has gradually, from very small beginnings, arrived at the prominent position it holds to-day. Possessed of very extensive premises fully equipped with all the modern improvements and appliances adapted to the trade, and conducted with exemplary honesty and straightforwardness, the firm enjoys the same excellent reputation as that obtained for their meats in all quarters where they are known. Orders are received daily from the United States, Great Britain, France and the West Indies. Amongst other distinctions obtained by their meats, may be mentioned a medal and diploma at the Colonial Exhibition held in London, England, and a gold medal and diploma the highest award at the Jamaica Exhibition.

Drawing Room, Hon. W. E. Sanford.

"Pinehurst," Residence of William Southam.

THE HAMILTON COTTON COMPANY.

The Hamilton Cotton Company was established in 1880, the proprietors being Messrs. R. A. Lucas and James M. Young. The mills are situated on Mary Street with a frontage of 250 feet, while many other premises occupy the ground at the back of the main mill. Over 200 people are steadily employed in manufacturing the various lines of goods produced by the mills. This company has obtained and enviable reputation throughout the entire country for the quality of their various products. The trade has steadily increased until it now extends from the Atlantic to the Pacific slope. Numerous medals at various exhibitions have been obtained, and its manufactures generally are held in the highest esteem. Excellent management and a thorough knowledge of the fabrics and their manufacture have led to these results. This company now represents one of the leading industries of the city, and has contributed very materially in giving to Hamilton its significance as the principal manufacturing centre in the Dominion.

Christ Church Cathedral.

Church or Ascension

St Thomas Church.

W. E. Sanford Manufacturing Co.

W. E. Sanford,

The warehouses of the W. E. Sanford Manufacturing Company are situated on the corner of King and John Streets having a frontage on the former street of 125 feet with a depth on the latter of over 150 feet.

This is the largest clothing establishment in the Dominion giving employment to probably three thousand persons. The volume of business reaches considerably over a million per annum, and its output is on the shelves of the best clothing and general store dealers in every province.

Travellers from the house visit the remotest as well as the more central parts of our broad Dominion.

In addition to the Hamilton headquarters, a branch of the house has been established at Winnipeg, and its warehouses there are a model of completeness and good taste. Agencies of the business are also to be found in Toronto, St. Johns, N. B., and Victoria, British Columbia.

The moving spirit of the concern, who originally founded the business and has remained at the head of it to the present, is the Hon. W. E. Sanford. His ability and enterprise have carried the business up from small proportions to its present extent and magnitude, and outside of his business, the impress of his energy has been felt in many directions for the general weal.

Mr. Sanford was called to a seat in the Dominion Senate, where his extensive experience and wide knowledge of our country have enabled him to render valuable assistance in the framing of its laws.

The Canada Bank of Commerce.

This bank, although its headquarters are in Toronto, has a number of shareholders among the citizens of Hamilton, and taking into account the large amount of business it transacts in this city and having bought out the old Gore bank it may well be considered largely a Hamilton institution. The bank was established in 1867—the birth year of Canadian Confederation, and in 1868 the Hamilton branch was opened.

The capital of the bank is $6,000,000, all paid up, and it has a reserve of $1,000,000. The simplest test of the position it has gained among its fellow institutions, is shown by the growth of its deposits. At the close of 1867 they amounted to $766,000; at the close of 1877, $7,304,000; while at the 31st of May, 1892, they have reached $17,000,184. The dividend paid this year is the fiftieth dividend and for the entire period of the bank's existence it has never failed to pay half-yearly dividends, the average being at the rate of about seven and three-quarters per cent. per annum on capital paid up and the aggregate of dividends paid amounts to the very large sum of $10,137,955.

The Canadian Bank of Commerce enters upon its second quarter-century with assets over $27,000,000. It has branches in Montreal and every city and Town of moment in Canada. The Hamilton branch is and has been for some years, under the management of D. Roberts, Esq., a most deservingly popular manager of great experience. It is quite safe to say that the business of the bank in Hamilton will grow and prosper, for among our manufacturers and merchants and farming community, there is not a monetary institution that enjoys a greater degree of confidence.

" Undercliffe," Residence of Wm. H. Gielard.

The Residence of a Merchant Prince.

"Wesanford," the magnificent residence of the Hon. W. E. Sanford, is situated at the corner of Jackson and Caroline Streets. The house is the old Jackson homestead, endeared to the heart of the present owner from his earliest childhood days. He has for more than two years been remodelling and rebuilding until, at the present time, a perfect palace is the result.

Senator Sanford's residence is, perhaps, the most beautiful home in the Dominion. Its contents are remarkable, for within its walls are contained a collection of works of art, statuary and paintings, gems of vertu, objects curious and beautiful, the result of six years' travel in all parts of Europe and many countries in this hemisphere, all chosen and collected with an artistic eye and with the sole object of beautifying and adorning his home seat.

In the construction of "Wesanford," is seen the same genius which in so short a time built up the most successful commercial enterprise of its kind in Canada. Everything in and around the house is of the most complete, most thorough and choice character.

The D. Moore Company (Limited).

This old and widely known firm was established in 1828 by Edward Jackson, who some years later, formed a partnership with the late Dennis Moore. In 1872 Mr. Jackson died, and Mr. Moore assumed full control of the business. The present joint stock company comprising the members of Mr. Moore's family, with W. A. Robinson as President, W. W. Robinson, vice-President and Ed. J. Moore, Secretary, was formed shortly after Mr. D. Moore's death, in November, 1887. The company is now one of the most extensive manufacturing concerns in the city, also being importers of and wholesale dealers in tin plate and Canada plate, sheet iron, sheet copper, galvanized iron, Russian iron, block tin, wire, etc. They also handle a full line of tinsmiths' tools and machines, pressed, stamped and spun ware, iron-clad milk-can fixtures, and general tinsmiths' trimmings in great variety. The building represented in the engraving is the office and show rooms, situated at 98, 100 King Street, east. These premises have been recently enlarged and improved, and are now most conveniently adapted, with modern facilities for their extensive trade. The foundry is situated at the corner of Catharine and Robert Streets, and here is manufactured the "Superior" line of superior stoves and ranges, hollow ware and general small wares in great variety, among which are the following : Saratoga range, for coal or wood; Mayflower cook, for coal or wood; Bermuda, Florida, Britannia, Winner and New Conqueror, wood cooks; Highlander and Queen, elevated oven, wood cooks; Loyal Canadian, high art square base burner and double heater, with and without oven; New Jewel, round base burner, with and without oven; Burlington, sheet iron

Cedar Grove, Residence of John Proctor.

Walter Woods & Co. Long and Bailey

surface burner and double heater with and without oven; Riverside Oak, the new and latest improvement in round hot blast double heaters, for coal or wood; Forest King and Forest Queen, round heaters, for coal or wood; Venus Franklin, open grate stove for coal; Sunbeam square parlor, and a general assortment of box stoves for wood, and the celebrated New Crown oil stove, in many styles.

John McPherson & Co.

At the corner of John and Jackson Streets may be seen the large boot and shoe manufactory of John McPherson & Co., one of the largest establishments in Canada and the largest in Ontario. The business is one of long standing, having been established in 1855, when the premises occupied were situated on King Street, east. With the growing demands of trade the firm was forced to vacate their much too small factory and erect the present large works. The success of this enterprising move is now more than assured. The new building has been occupied only two years, and the factory is running at its full capacity, having orders placed for months ahead. The trade covers the whole of the Dominion, and the standard quality of the goods manufactured, is well known among dealers.

It is no flattery but a bare statement of fact, to say that the goods turned out at this establishment are the very best in Canada. The person who has once tried a pair of McPherson's boots or shoes, will always ask for them again; a truth that has led all wideawake boot and shoe dealers in the country to keep this make in stock. The John McPherson & Co.'s stamp on a pair of shoes is as good a guarantee as any body needs.

"Rosearden," Residence of T. H. Pratt.

THE E. & C. GURNEY COMPANY (Limited).

Fifty years ago when Hamilton was but a poor insignificant place, and the iron industry represented by one small foundry, which has long since disappeared, the inauguration of the present vast and extensive business of the E. and C. Gurney Company took place. Commencing in a very small way, but sufficient for the needs of the town, the trade soon extended as Hamilton was opened up and the influx of settlers increased, till now it has assumed gigantic proportions with branch establishments in Toronto, Montreal, Winnipeg and Boston, Massachusetts. Commencing in small premises on John Street, Edward and Charles Gurney, with a staff consisting of one man and a boy, found that the output of a couple of stoves a day was quite equal to the demand, but affairs soon changed, population increased and Hamilton grew to such an extent, that it was soon found necessary to enlarge their premises, and increase the output of heating and cooking apparatus to keep up with the demand. One enlargement of the premises followed another, and it was even necessary to purchase a church and add it to the establishment. In 1860 the old foundry was pulled down and the present imposing edifice erected, and in 1875 it was still further improved by the erection of a handsome four-storied building consisting of offices and warehouse.

From the smallest beginning the E. & C. Gurney Company have become the largest industry of their kind in the Dominion. To Charles Gurney, the surviving brother, and to Edward Gurney, who passed away a few years ago, the city of Hamilton owes much. In the year 1883 the concern was incorporated under its present title, with E. Gurney as President, and C. Gurney, vice-President. The company manufactures cooking stoves, ranges, hot air furnaces and registers, agricultural furnaces and indeed, everything in the line. The E. & C. Gurney's reputation and manufactures are not confined to Canada and the United States alone, their system of heating having been introduced into the British Isles and London, more particularly where some of the largest Grand Opera Houses and places of entertainment are heated by their system and apparatus.

The Gurney Company are also the owners of the Gurney Ware Scale Works here— an establishment which is known all over the Dominion as manufacturers of weigh machines of every kind required in the country

The Hamilton business of the E. & C. Gurney firm is managed by Mr. John H. Tilden, a member of the firm—a thorough business man—a member of the City Council, an able financier, and active co-operator in connection with anything of interest to Hamilton.

MALCOLM AND SOUTER.

Manufacturers of fine furniture, and importers of and dealers in carpets, oil cloths and every description of house furnishings. They succeeded the well-known old established business of the late James Reed eight years ago. The firm employ forty men and ship their furniture to all parts of the Dominion.

Their premises are 91 and 93 King St., west. Mr. W. Malcolm and A. M. Souter were both born in Aberdeen. They are pushing energetic men, and have fitted up churches, ware, houses and offices from the extreme east to extreme west of Canada.

Provident Life Building.

John Calder & Co.

Copp Brothers

The Empire Foundry of which Messrs. Copp Brothers are the enterprising proprietors, occupies the large premises on the corner of York and Bay Streets. The business was originated in Woodstock many years ago, under the name of Copp, Finch and Copp; but when the business became the property of the Messrs. Copp, it migrated to Hamilton, where it has built up one of the most solid and substantial businesses in the city. Its turnout consists principally of stoves and ranges, English grates and enamelled ware. Messrs. Copp Brothers have of late been manufacturing hot air furnaces and registers which have largely added to its already very extensive business. Another feature of Messrs Copp Brothers' business is the manufacture of Agricultural implements which are known and widely used throughout Canada. Mr. William Copp is a public man who takes great personal interest in the affairs of the city. He is an ex-city councillor and a strong temperance advocate. In matters of religion again Mr. Copp is always to the fore, in fact it would be difficult to mention any matters of any moment at the present day in which Mr. Copp is not interested.

The Hamilton Bridge and Tool Company.

This company was formed in 1872, but was reorganized in 1880. Wm. Hendrie, Esq., is the President and John Stewart, Secretary-Treasurer. Their first order was the building the large swing railway bridge over the Burlington Canal in 1876, since which they have completed five hundred and one iron and steel structures of immense power for railways in every part of Canada. This company, last year, added to their business of bridge building that of iron and steel ships, and launched during the year a splendid new steamer—the "Arabian"—180 feet in length, and are at the present time building a steam yacht, 101⁴₈ feet long, 16 feet wide and 9 feet deep, for Mr. Albert G. Gooderham, and a large steel steamship, to be called the "Niagara"; length, 311 feet; width, 36 feet; depth of hold, 13½ feet. The iron shield work, forming the construction of the St. Clair tunnel, was all made by the Hamilton Bridge and Tool Company, under the special supervision of Mr. Telper, their Consulting Engineer.

Knox, Morgan & Co.

Previous to the railroad era in Ontario, Hamilton, being the head of navigation on Lake Ontario, held the lead in the Dry Goods trade, and so strong was her hold upon this trade that she maintained it many years after the building of railroads began to make lake and river navigation of less importance to the distributing trade of the country. Since the construction of the Great Western and Grand Trunk railways the vicissitudes of business have been strongly marked in the ambitious city. From 1850 to 1870 Hamilton boasted of such strong and favorably known dry goods houses as those of Buchanan, Harris & Co., Gordon, MacKay & Co., Young, Law & Co., A. & T. C. Kerr & Co., Kerr, Brown & McKenzie, D. MacInnes & Co., F. Gates & Co., and each of these houses claimed its share of the trade of the best portion of Ontario, that lying west of Toronto and south and west of Collingwood and Barrie, and a vast business in dry goods was done by the wholesale men of Hamilton.

The present leaders of the wholesale dry goods trade of Hamilton, are Knox, Morgan & Co. John Knox, formerly of Glasgow, is the senior member. After the death of A. Duncan, who was lost in the Asia disaster, September 14, 1882, Mr. Knox assumed control of the business, and the firm name was changed from A. Duncan & Co. to Knox, Morgan & Co. Mr. Knox's wide experience, general ability and industry are freely acknowledged by those with whom he has had business relations, and to him is given, by common consent, a foremost place among the business men of the ambitious city.

The other partner in this firm, Mr. Alfred Morgan, was thoroughly trained in the establishment of Buchanan, Harris & Co. He afterwards became connected with the firm of John I. MacKenzie & Co., (later A. Duncan & Co.), and it was during his connection with this firm that he was sent as representative to the British markets. He displayed unusual talent in the selection of goods, and soon began to be recognized as a first-class buyer. Long experience has given him a thorough acquaintance with the value of goods, and what is of more consequence, an intimate knowledge of the styles of dry goods suitable for Ontario. These qualifications, added to a thorough familiarity with the best markets for purchasing, places his firm on a par with the best in the Dominion. Successful dry goods merchants require higher training and greater skill and self-restraint than possibly those in any other business, to enable them not only to cater to but anticipate the ever varying wants of a fastidious public, who become more difficult to please and more versatile in their tastes from season to season.

Knox, Morgan & Co.'s establishment is situated on the south side of King street, immediately opposite Gore Park. It contains about 40,000 square feet of floorage, is conveniently laid out for the business, occupies a central position, and is in every way an attractive wholesale dry goods house. The light is perfect from the north and east, thus affording the greatest facility for inspecting the stock, while the arrangements for the display of goods make it easy and pleasant for buyers. Owing to the recent increase in business an hydraulic elevator greatly facilitates the handling of the goods.

The push and energy shown by this young house, with ample and steadily increasing capital, straight forward dealing and consideration for their customers, have placed them high among their competitors, their steady aim being to seek the trade and support of independent merchants by giving terms and prices and goods which enable their customers to meet honest competition and leave them ample profits.

The facilities possessed by them for handling colored cottons are exceptional, being in close proximity to the Ontario, Dundas Hamilton and Merritton cotton mills.

Twice each year the foreign markets are searched by representatives of the firm, when all the great mercantile and manufacturing centres of the United Kingdom, Germany, France, Switzerland and Austria, are regularly visited, and the choicest goods to be had are picked up direct from the manufacturers. The business is conducted on the departmental system, so large and carefully arranged that the constantly increasing volume of business can be expeditiously handled without the slightest friction or confusion.

Every detail is worked out under the supervision of tried and experienced heads of departments (some employés having been connected with the business in its different styles for twenty years), and customers can always confidently rely upon even their smallest order receiving the closest attention, and upon its being filled and the goods forwarded with promptitude.

DIXON BROS., WHOLESALE DEALERS IN FRUITS.

The firm of Dixon Brothers carry on an extensive business in fruits, and rank among the largest importers of foreign and exporters of domestic fruits in Canada. They have extensive premises on the south side of King street (East), very near to the general Post Office. The Bros. Dixon are energetic men of business, and are known all over the Dominion in connection with their line of business. They take an interest in all affairs for the benefit of Hamilton, and ready at all times to give a helping hand toward its advancement.

LEVY BROTHERS, WHOLESALE JEWELERS.

This house was founded in 1862 by Herman and Abraham Levy, who carried on business as H. & A. Levy, and the firm of to-day as Levy Bros. is perhaps the leading wholesale house of the kind in British North America.

Jewelry, Clocks, Watches, Jewelers' Materials, Watchmakers' Tools and Materials, Optical Goods of every description—it would be impossible to attempt a description of the hundreds, yes, thousands, of articles of jewelry in Gold, Silver, Jet and Plate displayed. The members of the firm have had a lifelong experience in the trade, and their energetic efforts have enabled them to extend their business to every corner of the Dominion. Men of sterling integrity, Hamilton has ever been proud of them.

HAMILTON BUSINESS COLLEGE.

Among the many and various scholastic institutions of Canada, the Hamilton Business College and Shorthand Institute is held in high repute. Established with the object of providing a first class commercial training for young people, it has become extremely popular with both sexes. Students are received from the age of fourteen and upwards, to all departments of the college, which include bookkeeping in all its forms, shorthand, typewriting, professional and business penmanship, French, German and other languages, drawing, etc. The college occupies very handsome and extensive premises, its different classes are largely attended, the fees being very moderate, and the value of the principles inculcated during a course of instruction are of incalculable benefit to the rising generation of business men and women in whatever branch of commerce or profession they may enter.

Norton Manufacturing Co.

Young Men's Christian Association.

The Young Men's Christian Association, which thrives so well in all the cities of Canada, was organized in 1867. It has had a great success from its inception, many of the leading citizens' names being found on its roll of officers and members.

The Association has erected for itself a substantial and commodious edifice, which with its internal arrangements has cost over $40,000. Its appointments include reading room, library, parlor, writing room, meeting room, secretary's office, a very good gymnasium, bath rooms, a large lecture and concert hall capable of seating about 900 people.

The Hamilton Field Battery.

The Hamilton Field Battery is the oldest Volunteer Artillery Corps in Ontario. For many years it was known as the Hamilton Volunteer Field Artillery, and was then what was in the early days called a "Cannon Company"; that is, an independent corps with a single field-piece. It was organized on its present footing in 1850. The equipment of the battery at present consists of four serviceable 9-pounder muzzle-loading rifle guns, with a full complement of harness and other stores. The battery consists of about eighty officers and men commanded by Major Henry Picton Van Wagner.

Bruce & Co.

W. H. Gellard & Co.

THE GRANT-LOTTRIDGE BREWING CO. (LIMITED).

There is no better known brewery in Canada than that of the Grant-Lottridge Brewing Co. (Limited) in this city. It is known as the Spring Brewery, and the ales and lager beer made here have a Dominion reputation.

The brewery is situated at the corner of Bay and Mulberry streets. The Spring Brewery is the oldest, having been established in 1842, and from a small beginning in the early days, when people were few in Hamilton, it has been gradually enlarged and developed until it is now not only able to supply nearly all the ale used in the city and a preponderating proportion of the lager used here, but it sends its products far and wide throughout the Dominion. The ale made by the Grant-Lottridge Brewing Co. (Limited) stands indisputably with the best of imported English ales.

The rapidity with which lager beer became a favorite beverage in this part of Canada only a few years ago, induced the Spring Brewery people to go into its manufacture, and they put in the very best modern plant. The most approved appliances are used in this department by a most skilled staff of lager beer brewers, and the result is a popular beverage of which an immense quantity is daily consumed. The product of this brewery has never, since the establishment of the business, been in any way cheapened or deteriorated by the use of substitutes or adulterants. The beer is a pure extract of malt and hops. No other ingredients are used in its manufacture. It is claimed that when the Grant-Lottridge Brewing Company's beer is drank it will invigorate and tone up the system much more efficaciously than the majority of widely advertised tonics, whose only claim to excellence is the fact that the principal constituents of Grant's beer are used in small amounts in their makeup.

The popularity of their ale and beer is largely to be attributed to the purity of the materials used and to the unvarying care exercised in its manufacture. This Company buy all their own barley under their own personal supervision from the best barley section of Canada, and have their own malt houses, in which only the highest grade of malt is made.

The brewery is supplied with all the modern appliances which science has placed at the disposal of the manufacturer, and it is safe to say that there is no establishment in the country better equipped or better supplied with facilities for a large production than this.

Lucas, Steele & Bristol.

The Grant-Lottridge Brewing Co.

THE THIRTEENTH BATTALION.

Composed of about 400 officers and men, the thirteenth battalion is the pride of Hamilton. Well equipped, well disciplined, with a most efficient Commandant (Colonel the Honorable I. M. Gibson) and staff of officers, the battalion, when it turns out on a field day, would do credit to the finest regiment of the line. The Dominion Government erected a handsome and commodious structure for their headquarters at a cost of $75,000, fitted with every modern convenience, the drill hall affording accommodation for over 3,000 people, who often assemble to listen to the splendid band, which has not its equal in the Dominion and certainly no finer one exists on the American Continent. It is in great requisition both at home and abroad, making annual trips to such places as Buffalo, Chicago, Detroit and Denver cities, in the United States, and all the principal cities in the Dominion. It is about 26 years since this famous band was organized, and for over 20 years it has been under the able control of the present popular bandmaster, Mr. George Robinson. At the triennial conclave of Knights Templar, held at St. Louis, in 1886, out of 150 bands present the Thirteenth Band and Gilmore's were the only ones chosen to play as solo bands, the whole 150 afterwards joining in a burst of harmony. This was an honor thoroughly appreciated in Hamilton and throughout Canada.

'E. & C. Gurney & Co.

THE LORETTO CONVENT.

The Loretto Convent, surrounded by extensive grounds, is situated on the corner of King and Ray streets. It was founded in the year 1866 by the mother establishment in Toronto. The objects of the convent are scholastic, teaching young ladies from about the age of five years until their education is completed. The higher education of women is one of the momentous questions of the present day; and as an educational establishment and training school in Art, Music and Modern languages, and the preparation of those who propose to graduate as teachers, the Loretto Convent has obtained a great and well deserved reputation. It is distinctly high class in all respects, the daughters of some of the best families in and around Hamilton having been educated within its walls. It is Roman Catholic, but the benefits to be derived from it are enjoyed by all sects and denominations; all are allowed liberty to adhere to the tenets of their own faith. Boarders to the number of fifty are received at the Convent, which has also a day school attached, attended by an average of over one hundred pupils who are carefully looked after by the lady superior and an able staff of assistants. A large addition to the Convent is now being contemplated, comprising an Examination Hall and Dormitories, which when completed will make the Loretto Convent one of the most desirable places of educational resort in Canada.

J. WINER & Co., WHOLESALE DRUGGISTS.

The late senior partner of this firm, whose name it still bears, settled in Hamilton in 1829 and established the drug business the following year, and it has continued uninterruptedly for now sixty-two years. In 1857 the partnership was formed as J. Winer & Co., and continued, with slight change of personnel, till January, 1884, when Mr. Winer retired, the firm retaining the old name. In 1862 the retail department of the business was sold out, and since that time it has been exclusively wholesale.

The buildings occupied and owned by this firm are four stories in height, and form the handsome structure on King Street (East) and not far from the Post Office and all our banking institutions, and extends back to Main Street, there facing the Court House. The name of J. Winer & Co. is a household word with every druggist in the Province.

The members of the firm are all practical men who have obtained a wide knowledge of every requirement of the trade, and they know the best markets of the world in which to purchase goods; they therefore possess the best facilities for supplying their customers with the very best and purest of every article required, and have always been noted as giving the best possible value to those who are fortunate enough to be customers of the firm.

Hamilton Cotton Co.

Oak Hall, James Street, North.

The Oak Hall Clothing House is unique in itself in Hamilton, inasmuch as the stock is all made especially for it by the leading wholesale clothing manufacturing company of the Dominion. The goods are cut in the most fashionable styles, and extra care is taken in the makeup. The building is three stories high, with full plate glass front and solid oak flooring. The shelving and ranges of tables on both the first and second flats are also of solid oak.

Wesleyan Ladies' College.

Situated on King street East, is a grand five story building of composite style of architecture, with Corinthian pillars. Established in 1861, it has had a noble career, having educated over three thousand young ladies, its graduates numbering two hundred and fifty. The building contains one hundred and fifty rooms besides magnificent parlors and bathrooms. Its ceilings are high, halls wide, and extensive playgrounds in the rear, thus insuring to its pupils everything, conducive and necessary to recreation and health. The course of study is the most comprehensive of its kind, embracing music, all modern languages, and all the arts and sciences. Its faculty includes over twenty highly accomplished ladies and gentlemen, and is presided over by Rev. A. Burns, D.D., LL.D., who fills the office of Governor and Principal. As the head of this splendid institution the principal is exceedingly popular.

While the name of the college is denominational, its doors are open to all, and its graduates and pupils belong to all religions. Higher education of the young ladies is the sole aim of the institution, and while strictest watch is kept over the conduct of pupils by Mrs. Burns and her assistants they are in no wise convent-bound or biased by creed or theory. Culture in all that is beautiful and useful is the one aim of the college.

Elsinore.

A building erected by the Hon. W. E. and Mrs. Sanford at the beach, and by them dedicated for the sick and suffering little ones of Hamilton.

The building is designed and constructed after the style of summer resorts and presents a handsome appearance. Its total length is 124 feet and its width 48 feet.

Complete the buildings cost $10,000.00 and nothing was spared to make this one of the most complete structures of the kind to be found in the country. The grounds are 140 feet wide and 214 feet in length.

The children's dormitories are the beau ideal of neatness and comfort. The rooms are lofty, airy and well lighted. The little cots with snow white counterpanes, soft beds and the gold and blue iron framework, look tempting enough for any wearied little one's peaceful slumbers.

" In as much as ye did it unto one of these, ye did it unto Me."

Poor sick and orphaned ones who know nothing of what Dryden calls " intervals of bliss."

" Little children climbing for a kiss,
    Welcome their father's late return at night."

The Eagle Knitting Co.

This company's factory is situated on the corner of Main and McNab Streets. It is a brick building, 150 x 50 ft., four stories high.

About two hundred hands are employed. The machines are run by steam power and the building is lighted by electricity, generated by the Co.'s dynamo on the premises. The goods, made for men, women and children, are known as *the Hygiene Underwear*, and are to be found in every town in Canada, from the Atlantic to the Pacific.

Balfour & Co., Wholesale Grocers and Importers.

This live and energetic firm is really a continuation of the old firms of W. D. McLaren & Co., Brown, Gillespie & Co., Brown, Routle & Co. and Brown, Balfour, Jr.

They do a large and growing business throughout Western Ontario and Manitoba and the Northwest Territories. Their customers know they will be treated squarely and honestly, and do not hesitate to order by letter at open prices even car lots of goods.

Their premises are very central, and are commodious and thoroughly adapted for their business.

The Meriden Brittania Works.

Hamilton Agricultural Works

Robert Evans & Co.

This firm of wholesale and retail seedsmen, whose premises we engrave on another page, was established by Mr. Robert Evans, the sole guiding spirit, in 1870. Ever since its inception the business has steadily increased until it has become one of the leading establishments of the kind in Canada. Wherever there is a farm or a garden, or a lover of flowering bulbs and plants, the name of Robert Evans is a household word, and ample guarantee for the name, germinating qualities, and value of the seeds sent out.

Progression, experience and sound judgment are leading characteristic elements in Mr. Evans' life, whether as a merchant or a citizen; hence the growth and success of the establishment in every possible direction. In commercial dealings, the firm has not confined itself to local or even Canadian fields, but has carried its export operations in field seeds, blue grass, clover, timothy grasses of all kinds into England, Ireland, Scotland, France, Germany, etc., where the firm is well known among the leading seed buyers of Europe, while throughout the United States it has a most extensive trade. Mr. Evans has been largely instrumental in introducing and increasing the adoption of ensilage corn into Canada, and many leading and now well-known varieties of wheat, barley, oats, field and garden vegetables are due to his indomitable perseverance and wise forethought.

Mr. Robert Evans has identified himself as one of Hamilton's leading citizens, in every way tending to enhance the wealth and prosperity of the city. He has held many public offices and has served as a city alderman. Politically he has ever been to the front as a staunch local and patriotic supporter of the present government. In social circles his heart and hand are ever ready to assist whenever help or duty requires them. Indeed it may be said that the city of Hamilton is undoubtedly and justly proud that its long civic roll of honorable, trusty and leading servants has also inscribed thereon the well-known seed firm of " Robert Evans & Co."

THE FEDERAL LIFE ASSURANCE COMPANY.

Their splendid premises are on James Street, north—a large solid stone structure, originally built for the Bank of Upper Canada.

The Federal Life is one of our monetary institutions to be proud of. Established in 1882, it has paid over half a million to policyholders during the past five years, has a sum assured of eleven millions, and a surplus to policyholders of $686,390.84.

Copp Bros. & Co.

Laidlaw Manufacturing Co.

The Federal is one of the most prosperous institutions in the Province. The management is careful and energetic. The invested assets of the company are represented by first class securities. To every one interested in life assurance (and who is not?) should make a study of the Federal's report of 1892; they are convincing statements and figures. The assurance business done is confined to Canada only, and its agencies are established from Halifax, in Nova Scotia, to Vancouver, in British Columbia. It is a credit to the company that its board aims to keep expenses low, and does not propose to pay too much for business —a safe company, which has the confidence of the people of the Dominion.

Mr. James H. Beatty is President; Mr. Wm. Kerns, M.P.P., and Mr. A. Burns, LL.D., Vice-Presidents; Mr. David Dexter, Managing Director.

JOHN A. BRUCE & CO., SEED MERCHANTS.

The Seed Warehouse of this firm, which is one of the largest and best equipped in Canada, is situated on the corner of King and McNab Streets, has a frontage of 30 feet on the former and 130 feet on the latter, occupying seven plots. The business was established by John A. Bruce in 1850, and in 1861 his brother, F. C. Bruce, became partner. A steadily increasing trade during the forty-two years' existence of this house is an evidence that careful supervision

Burrow, Stewart & Milne.

Robert Evans & Co.

has not been wanting to create this success, which has developed in proportion with the rapid and extraordinary growth of the country's Railway System.

The demand for Bruce's seeds come as regularly as the Spring, and from every portion of the Dominion between the Atlantic and Pacific Oceans, and it is not confined to the Continent alone, as the firm are large exporters of clover seeds, grass seeds and garden peas to Britain, France, Germany and the United States, and at time of writing this notice two carloads of Alaska clover seeds and one of Canadian blue grass are being prepared for foreign shipment, and the preparation of the system of cleaning the seed by fanning mills specially adapted for

James Turner & Co.

The Freeman Block.

the purpose, and driven by electricity, are features worthy of notice, and the systematic arrangement of thousands of bags of seeds distributed through their extensive establishment give evidence of the magnitude.

HAMILTON PROVIDENT AND LOAN COMPANY, HAMILTON.

The Hamilton Provident and Loan Society was established in June, 1871, and is to-day one of the most popular, successful and useful institutions in the Dominion of Canada. It combines the functions of a building society and savings bank, in the latter department the deposits ranging considerably over a million dollars yearly. Its directors are gentlemen well known all over Canada for their influence, enterprise and sterling worth. The building is one of the best in the city, four stories high, built of the best quality of Ohio stone. The banking office is one of the most handsome and complete in every respect, the fittings of massive walnut, richly carved with panels of cut glass. The floor inlaid with Minton tiles. The board room is finished with butternut in oil; the furniture is walnut, covered with red morocco leather. The capital is over a million and a half, and the management excellent in every respect.

Gurney & Ware

THE FIRE DEPARTMENT.

In no other city in the Dominion are fires so insignificant as in Hamilton, and if there is one institution the people of Hamilton are more proud of than another it is its splendid fire department, under its energetic and efficient chief, Alexander W. Aitchison. The department has arrived at a state of efficiency bordering on perfection. When the fire alarm rings out it is one of the sights of Hamilton to see the brigade sweep past at lightning speed, headed by its popular chief. To the chief the men are devoted and would sacrifice anything at his bidding. He is not the man to order another to do what he himself would not risk doing, and his men know it, hence the *esprit du corps* that exists amongst them from highest to lowest. One of the secrets of there being so few serious conflagrations lies in the fact of the department receiving the earliest possible information of any outbreak of fire, telephone stations being placed in all quarters of the city communicating directly with the headquarters station.

The central fire premises are well worthy of a visit by strangers to the city, and if they are lucky enough to see the horses "hitch to" and the brigade turn out, they will have seen something worth traveling for. The brigade now numbers about fifty officers and men, and its equipment is in every respect equal to all and any demands that may be made upon the department.

The Ontario Rolling Mills and Nail and Forging Works.

These extensive works, which were established by American capitalists in 1879, comprise a number of large buildings and cover several acres. The main buildings are three in number, viz:

The Rolling Mill, 200 ft. square.
The Nail Factory, 175 x 60 ft.
The Forging Works, 160 ft. square.

They are all equipped with the most modern machinery for the manufacture of Iron and Steel Sheet Plates, Merchant Bar and Band Iron, Tire, Sleigh Shoe and Bar Steel, Fish Plates, Iron, Steel and Clinch Nails, Spikes, Rivets and Washers, heavy and light Forgings of Iron and Steel, &c.

The reader will glean some idea of the magnitude of these works by the following facts: The machinery is run by fourteen steam engines of fifteen hundred horse power in the aggregate; three large pumps for bringing the water from the bay for mill purposes; two duplex pumps for feeding the boilers, of which there are sixteen; five mill trains, two 20 in., one 14 in., one 10 in. and one 9 in., with adequate furnaces for each; several steam hammers, the largest of which strikes a blow of twenty tons; forty automatic nail and five washer and rivet cutting machines, &c.

In the Forging Works there are three Cranes, one made of iron capable of carrying fifteen tons. Our space forbids further enumeration. There is also a large Machine Shop where all the tools used are made. 550 hands are employed.

Thistle Rink.

THE GERMANIA CLUB

Was organized in October, 1871, under the name of Gesangverein Germania. The Society occupied various halls up to the year 1874, when it was necessary, owing to the progress it had made and the steady increase of members, to procure larger quarters, since which time, with the exception of two years, it has occupied the old Masonic Hall on the corner of Main and John Streets. In 1874 the Society joined the Canadian German Saengerbund, which was then organized. On June 30th, 1881, the Society was incorporated as the "Germania Club" and on October 18th, 1884, the Club was also incorporated under the "Ontario Joint Stock Companies' Act." Rapid progress is the order in connection with the Club, and the co-operation of the ladies was secured by the efforts made from time to time for their entertainment. A library, piano, and other adjuncts were acquired and a stage built in the hall for the purpose of dramatic representations. The Club has progressed and has at all times maintained a good reputation among the citizens of Hamilton.

Knox, Morgan & Co.

JOHN MOODIE & SONS, FANCY GOODS EMPORIUM, 16 KING STREET, WEST.

This handsome establishment, which has a frontage of 24 ft. by 90 deep, four story, is the principal one of the kind in Hamilton. A heavy stock of every description of Fancy Goods in endless variety. Silverware, Toys, Ladies' Underwear, Berlin and other Wools, and the many knick-knacks required by ladies.

The business was started in a small way in 1856 by Mr. John Moodie and has gradually increased to its present mammoth dimensions. The goods on each flat are tastefully arranged in what may be termed the Fancy Bazaar of Ontario.

Bowes, Jameson & Co.

Archdale Wilson & Co.   T. B. Greening & Co.

Bowman Hardware Co.

The Bank of Hamilton.

Established twenty years ago by a few energetic and far seeing business men of the city, the Bank of Hamilton has made such progress that it now occupies a high and proud position among the great monetary institutions of the country. The president, John Stuart, A. G. Ramsay, the vice-president, the other officers and board of directors, represent some of the wealthiest establishments in the city, and are all men known far and wide for their unswerving integrity and business qualifications. Under this board works a staff of clear headed gentlemen, trained to the banking profession, careful and shrewd and eminently successful in the performance of their duties. Mr. J. Turnbull, cashier, is the chief executive officer, and is ably seconded by the assistant cashier, Mr. H. S. Steven.

The paid up capital of the bank now amounts to a million and a quarter dollars, with a reserve fund of six hundred and fifty thousand, and total assets close on eight millions. The bank has established several agencies in the Province, and has its correspondents in England and the principal cities of the United States. The dividends for many years past have been eight (8) per cent.

What a thoroughly good local bank can contribute to the building up and sustaining a home industry has been significantly illustrated in the career of this institution. Starting out with a long list of the best and most successful business men of Hamilton as its share holders, the Bank of Hamilton received and has ever since enjoyed the confidence of the entire community. In 1881 John Stuart, Esq., was elected president, and has been re-elected at each annual meeting ever since. The magnificent Bank Building, recently erected, is situate at the southwest corner of King and James Streets, built of brown stone, and handsomely fitted up with every modern convenience.

W. H. Gillard & Co.

The prosperity attending the firm of W. H. Gillard & Co. affords striking proof that success is the child of energy wedded to intelligence. Perfect mastery of detail, intimate knowledge of the needs of the public, quick adaptation to improved methods, close application to business, and the adoption of a broad, liberal policy in the general conduct of their business are among the factors which have contributed in placing this firm in the front rank of the wholesale grocery trade of Canada.

Founded in 1879 by Mr. W. H. Gillard (previously prominently connected for twenty-one years with the wholesale grocery trade) and Mr. John Gillard, the firm quickly established its trade in Ontario, Manitoba, British Columbia and the Northwest Territories. In 1884 Mr. H. N. Kittson was taken into the partnership, and year by year the area of their business has steadily increased. In 1885 the firm found it necessary, in order to meet the requirements of their trade, to erect the handsome and capacious building which they now occupy on Main street, West. The present methods of conducting business afford few opportunities for the contact of principals with their patrons, and the commercial traveler becomes an important factor in the transaction of business. In recognition of this fact Messrs. W. H. Gillard & Co. are careful to be represented by gentlemen whose experience, integrity and tact are calculated to earn for them the confidence of the business public.

Mr. W. H. Gillard, the senior of the firm, although still a young man and in the prime and vigor of life, has been for thirty-five years identified with the wholesale grocery trade. He

Commercial Block.

is conspicuous for his public spirit and his identification with all projects having as their aim the advancement and development of the trade of the City of Hamilton. He has filled many public positions with ability and advantage to the public.

Mr. John Gillard's practical knowledge and his keen judgment of values have contributed much to the general prosperity of this firm, and his thorough knowledge of teas and the careful study and attention devoted by him to this important branch of the grocery trade account in a great measure for the large and steadily increasing volume of their tea trade.

Mr. H. N. Kittson is charged with the management of the financial affairs of the firm. His experience, discernment and well known enterprise and energy stamp him as being well equipped for his important duties.

With such a combination of business experience and energy it is not surprising that this firm has so steadily grown in favor with the trade, so that to-day the name of W. H. Gillard & Co. is accepted the Dominion over as synonymous with fair and honorable dealing.

Police Force.

The Hamilton Police Force, at the head of which is Chief Hugh McKinnon, is few in numbers but thoroughly efficient and well disciplined. It consists of only fifty men, but this number has been found amply sufficient for the requirements of the City, where serious crime is practically unknown and misdemeanors of all kinds extremely limited. The Chief is one of the

The Window of C. S. Cochran, Photographer.

most experienced detective officers in the Dominion and is fortunate enough to possess the entire confidence of his men, by whom he is ably seconded.

The Police Force is administered by three Commissioners, one of whom is the Mayor, another the Police Magistrate, and the third the Judge of the County Court. Generally speaking the Police Force of Hamilton is composed of a fine, athletic and intelligent body of men who know their duty thoroughly and do it every time.

J. HOODLESS & SON, MANUFACTURERS OF FINE FINISHED FURNITURE (Established 1850).

The factory and lumber yard of this well known firm occupy the whole of the block on Catherine Street from Main to Jackson Street, 400 ft. by 150 ft. wide. It is equipped with the most modern woodworking machinery, which is driven by a thirty horse power engine. The factory is lighted by electricity, the firm using its own dynamo. About fifty hands are employed constantly on full time all the year round.

The warehouse and warerooms are situated at Nos. 61, 63 and 65 King Street, West (*see illustration*). In these are displayed exquisite designs in Parlor, Dining and Bedroom furniture. A specialty is the manufacture of odd art chairs, of which there are over one hundred original designs, and for which Messrs. J. Hoodless & Son have become noted. Orders are daily received from all parts of Ontario, Quebec and Manitoba, for these works of art.